Praise for *The Orphan Choir*

'This bestselling thriller writer knows how to pile on the tension… and her ending is chillingly, memorably disturbing'
Culture Magazine, *Sunday Times*

'A creepy, tension-filled surprise. Part of a line of horror novellas produced by the Hammer/Arrow Books partnership, *The Orphan Choir* reveals a new aspect to Hannah's writing: she has proven her innovative skills in the form of psychological suspense multiple times; turns out she's no slouch when it comes to conjuring up ghostly presences either.'
Independent on Sunday

'This is an old-fashioned horror story, given a modern spin by the likeable narrator. It has a creepy cinematic feel and races along to its frightening ending.'
Sunday Mirror

'A chilling ghost story'
Saturday Magazine, *Daily Express*

'A very modern sort of ghost story…there's nothing like ghostly children to give you the collywobbles'
i, Independent

'For me, it's Sophie Hannah's *The Orphan Choir*, with its darker undertones and slow-building finale, that really steals the spotlight… Her subtle clues build up to bring the book to a powerful climax…a truly chilling read'
Stylist Magazine

Sophie Hannah is the internationally bestselling author of eight psychological thrillers, the most recent of which is *The Carrier*. Her crime novels featuring Simon Waterhouse and Charlie Zailer have been published in more than 25 countries, and adapted for ITV1 as *Case Sensitive*, starring Olivia Williams and Darren Boyd. In 2012, Sophie's novel *Kind of Cruel* was shortlisted for the Specsavers National Book Awards Crime Thriller of the Year, and in 2007 she was shortlisted for the TS Eliot Prize for her latest poetry collection, *Pessimism for Beginners*. She is a Fellow Commoner of Lucy Cavendish College, Cambridge, and her website is www.sophiehannah.com.

Also available by Sophie Hannah

Sophie Hannah

the orphan choir

HAMMER
AN EXCLUSIVE MEDIA COMPANY

Published by Arrow Books in association with Hammer 2013

2 4 6 8 10 9 7 5 3

First published in Great Britain in 2013 by
Arrow Books in association with Hammer

Random House, 20 Vauxhall Bridge Road,
London SW1V 2SA

www.randomhouse.co.uk

Addresses for companies within The Random House Group Limited can be found
at: www.randomhouse.co.uk/offices.htm

The Random House Group Limited Reg. No. 954009

A CIP catalogue record for this book
is available from the British Library

ISBN 9780099580027

The Random House Group Limited supports the Forest Stewardship
Council® (FSC®), the leading international forest-certification organisation. Our
books carrying the FSC label are printed on FSC®-certified paper. FSC is the only
forest-certification scheme supported by the leading environmental organisations,
including Greenpeace. Our paper procurement policy
can be found at: www.randomhouse.co.uk/environment

Typeset by SX Composing DTP, Rayleigh, Essex
Printed and bound by CPI Group (UK) Ltd, Croydon, CR0 4YY

the
orphan
choir

The liturgical responses in this book come from real choral services I have attended at St Catherine's College in Cambridge — a wholly wonderful and non-spooky institution whose girls' choir, through no fault of its own, planted the seeds of a spooky story in my mind.

Vouchsafe, O Lord,
To keep us this night without sin.

O Lord, have mercy upon us,
Have mercy upon us.

O Lord, let thy mercy be upon us:
As our trust is in thee.

Turn us again, thou God of hosts:
Show the light of thy countenance, and we shall be whole.

O Lord, hear our prayer;
And let our cry come unto thee.

The Lord be with you;
And with thy spirit.

Let us pray.

Give us light in the night season we beseech thee, O Lord,
and grant that what we sing and say with our lips we may believe in
our hearts
and what we believe in our hearts we may show forth in our daily life
through Jesus Christ our Lord.
Amen.

ONE

September, October

I

It's quarter to midnight. I'm standing in the rain outside my next-door neighbour's house, gripping his rusted railings with cold wet hands, staring down through them at the misshapen and perilously narrow stone steps leading to his converted basement, from which noise is blaring. It's my least favourite song in the world: Queen's 'Don't Stop Me Now'.

There's a reddish-orange light seeping out into the darkness from the basement's bay window that looks as unappealing as the too-loud music sounds. Both make me think of hell: my idea of it. There are no other lights on anywhere in my neighbour's four-storey home.

My lower ground floor next door is dark and silent. We mainly use it as guest accommodation, and as we don't often have guests it is usually empty. It comprises two bedrooms, a playroom-cum-Xbox room for Joseph, and a large bathroom. All of number 19's internal cellar walls have been knocked down to make a single, vast area: either a chill-out den or an entertaining space, depending on whether you're talking to my neighbour or his girlfriend.

I think the label 'entertaining space' worries him because of its public-spirited implications. The word 'entertain' suggests that one might give a toss about people other than oneself. My next-door neighbour doesn't.

Freddy Mercury's reflections about supersonic women are making me glad that I've never met one: they sound like a bit of a handful — not very easy-going. I've never had ambitions in the direction of supersonicness, whatever it might be. What I want is far more achievable, I hope: to be warm, dry, asleep. At the moment, those are the only things I want, the only things I can imagine ever wanting.

The stairs leading from the pavement down to number 19's basement are slimy with moss, rain and street gunge. Each step's surface was a perfect rectangle once, but more than a hundred years' worth of feet and weather have worn away corners and edges, making them too uneven to use safely, especially in tonight's waterfall-style downpour. Normally I look at them and feel a twinge of satisfaction. The woman who sold us number 17 had recently had all of its eroded stonework replaced. The steps from our lower ground level up to the street are beautifully straight-edged, with a new black-painted iron handrail bolted on to them for added safety, but what does that matter, really? If I can't sleep in my house when I want to, all its other virtues are somewhat redundant.

Number 19 has no handrail. I don't fancy attempting the descent while water cascades from one step down to the next like a liquid Slinky toy without boundaries, but what choice do I have? If I want to get my neighbour's attention, I'll have to put myself where he can see me, or wait for a gap between songs and bang on the window of the room that he and his friends are in. I've rung the front doorbell seven times and he can't hear me. Of course he can't; Freddie Mercury is drowning out all other sounds.

I'm wearing pink-and-white checked pyjamas, drenched from knee to ankle, a black raincoat and trainers that were waterlogged five seconds after I left the house. My feet now feel as if they're in two flotation tanks, weighing me down. It's the opposite of people putting slabs of concrete in their pockets to make them sink when they wade into water; I am weighed down by water, on the pavement's concrete. This is the kind of rain the skies pour over your head in a never-ending torrent. It's hard to believe it's composed of light individual drops.

I can't help laughing at the absurdity of it as Freddie Mercury invites me to give him a call if I want to have a good time. The problem is that my definition of a good time differs greatly from the song's, and from Mr Fahrenheit's. That's what Stuart and I privately call our neighbour, though his real name is Justin Clay, and I've heard his friends and his girlfriend Angie call him Jub. My definition of a good time is being able to get into bed whenever I want to — yes, even quite early on a Saturday night — and for there to be no pounding rock anthems booming through my wall, preventing me from getting to sleep.

It only happens every two or three Saturdays.

Thankfully, Mr Fahrenheit spends at least every other weekend at Angie's house, but when her kids are with their dad, Angie comes to stay at number 19 and it's party time – or at least, it sounds to me like a party whenever it happens. Sometimes they decide to make the most of their child-free weekends and play loud music on two consecutive nights, Friday and Saturday. Mr Fahrenheit assures me that it is never a party, always a 'little get-together'. I have tried on four separate occasions to explain to him that I don't mind what we agree to call it as long as he's willing to lower the volume of his music to an acceptable level.

The get-together guests are always the same – the man who wears walking boots with the laces untied and tucks his jeans into his chunky socks; the stooped, too-tall man with the floppy hair and the rucksack; the frizzy-haired chain-smoking dance teacher who works at the performing arts school on Woolnough Road; the fat woman with red glasses and oddly sculpted hair dyed the colour of a blue Persian cat – and Mr Fahrenheit always plays the same songs for them to sing and shout along to, though, to be fair, he does vary the order: '9 to 5' by Dolly Parton, 'Livin' on a Prayer' by Bon

Jovi, Blondie's 'Heart of Glass', A-ha's 'Take on Me', 'Love Shack' by the B-52's, 'Video Killed the Radio Star' – I can't remember who that one's by.

And the centrepiece of his every musical gathering: 'Don't Stop Me Now' by Queen, which expresses my noisy neighbour's attitude to life far better than he himself does. I'm sure he hasn't analysed the lyrics as I have, but I don't think it can be a coincidence that he is a ruthlessly selfish hedonist and the song he blasts out more often than any other – usually two or three times on a party night – is a hymn to his ideology. The narrator in the song is not merely someone who wishes to have a good time (which would be reasonable) but someone who is acutely aware that the fun he intends to have (out of control, like an atom bomb) will adversely affect others to the point that they will find it unbearable and seek to put a stop to it. He anticipates this, and makes it clear that he only wants to hear from those who agree with him about what constitutes a good time.

Stuart would say – has said, often – that it's only a song and I'm reading too much into it. The inaccuracy of the criticism irritates me. The menacing lyrics are there for anyone and everyone to hear; there's nothing ambiguous about them. Stuart would be closer to the truth if he accused me not of finding meaning in the words that isn't there, but of imagining that 'Don't Stop Me Now' is more than a song, which is of course scientifically impossible.

Unscientifically, it is the putrid essence of Justin Clay, encapsulated in music. His soul made pop.

Finally, Queen's rant-with-a-tune ends. This is my chance. I know from experience that one song never follows swiftly on from another on these evenings. Efficient DJ'ing is not one of Mr Fahrenheit's strengths. I used to think that the long gaps between musical assaults were his sadistic attempt to lull me into a false sense of security in order to blast me again just as I'm nodding off, but that was unfair of me. I underestimated how long it takes to transfer the various ingredients of an unrolled spliff from a lap to a coffee table without mislaying any of them, especially while stoned, and then shuffle over to the stereo and make a decision about what to play next.

Now that the music's stopped, I can hear muffled voices, though I can't make out what they're saying over the drumming of the rain. Carefully, I make my way down the stone staircase backwards so that

I can hold on to the steps above me as I go. Once at the bottom, I turn and find Angie, the girlfriend, looking at me through the window, which, tonight, is a water feature. 'Jub, the lady from next door's here again,' she says after a few seconds of mute staring, as if shock has delayed her reaction. She's wearing a short green-and-white dress – fabric inspired by a lava lamp, by the look of it – with a longer beige knitted cardigan over it. Bare feet.

'Oh, you are giving me the *joke!*' Mr Fahrenheit cries out. I resist the temptation to ask him if that expression is popular in the playground at the moment. He's bent over his music system, his back to the window. At this proximity, I can hear him easily thanks to the single glazing. He's in no hurry to turn round and engage with me.

Neither he nor Angie seems to have grasped basic cause and effect. They know that I object to their playing of loud music late at night because I've told them so unequivocally, yet they seem surprised when they do it and I turn up at their house to complain. It's clear every time that they have not anticipated my arrival. Afterwards, I can't help pointlessly reciting to Stuart the conversation they must regularly fail to have:

You know, if she can't sleep because of our music, she'll need to find something else to do to fill up her night. What if that something else is coming round here and giving us a hard time?

Oh, yeah. I see your point. I'd say that's pretty likely to happen, since it's what always happens. If we don't like her coming round and moaning, maybe we shouldn't prevent her from sleeping.

Mr Fahrenheit walks over, opens the window, stands well back from the rain. 'Hello, Louise,' he says, his voice as sullen and weary as his face. 'Come to give me a bollocking?'

I try not to feel hurt, and fail. Was I secretly hoping he'd say, 'Come and join us, grab yourself a drink?' I think I might have been, stupid and naive though it undoubtedly is. I've often thought that if I can't sleep and there happens to be a party going on next door, I could do worse than join in and try to have some fun. I'd have to decline, of course, even if Mr Fahrenheit were to invite me.

I wonder if he knows that I would gladly stop hating him and be ready, even, to like him a bit if he would only show me a tiny bit of consideration.

'I find my midnight visits as inconvenient as you do, Justin,' I tell him. 'Especially when it's cold and the rain's bucketing down. Are you finished playing music now? It's nearly midnight.'

'No, I'm not *finished* playing music.' He sways backwards.

'Tell her to fuck off,' his walking-boot friend calls out, waving at me from his cross-legged position on the floor next to a free-standing lamp that's as tall as he is, seated, and has what looks like a red tablecloth draped over it. He and the lamp are two islands in a sea of empty wine bottles on their sides. The room looks as if a couple of dozen games of Spin the Bottle have been abandoned in a hurry.

I say to Justin, 'In that case, can you please keep the volume low from now on, so that it doesn't travel through the wall to my house?'

The fat woman with the red glasses appears at Mr Fahrenheit's side. 'Be reasonable, love,' she says. 'It's not midnight yet. Midnight's the cut-off point, isn't it? It is where I live. You've got to admit, you sometimes try to shut us down as early as quarter to eleven.'

'And Justin often plays his music until at least one-thirty,' I say. 'Why don't you encourage *him* to be reasonable? If I've come round before eleven it's because that's when I've wanted to go to sleep.'

'God's sake, Louise, it's fuckin' Saturday night,' Mr Fahrenheit protests.

'I sometimes go to bed early on Saturdays, and stay up late on Tuesdays,' I tell him. 'What if I was an airline pilot, and had to get up at four in the morning to—' I bring my sentence to an emergency stop, not wanting to give Mr Fahrenheit the chance to tell me I'm not an airline pilot and imagine he's proved me wrong. 'Look, all I want is to be able to go to bed when I want and sleep uninterrupted by your noise. *Please*, Justin.' I put on my best friendly, hopeful smile.

He raises his hands and backs away from me, as if I've got a gun pointed at him: one he knows isn't loaded. 'Louise . . . I'd like you to *fuck* off back home now, if you wouldn't mind. You've spoiled my evening again, like you've spoiled I don't know how many evenings – well done. Nice one. I'm not wasting any more of my time arguing with you, so . . . go home, or argue with yourself, whichever you'd prefer.'

'Chill out, next-door neighbaaah!' the man with the floppy fringe yells at me from the far side of the room. He's sitting at the big dining table that's dotted with torn Rizla packets and wine stains.

SOPHIE HANNAH

The table stands directly beneath the elaborate glass chandelier, pushed up against the room's only wallpapered wall. The paper is pale blue with gold violin-shaped swirls all over it. It's beautiful, actually, and was probably expensive, but brings on eye-ache if you look at it for too long. Mr Fahrenheit cares a lot about interior design. He cares equally about getting drunk and high, and not at all about tidying up. His house is an odd mixture of two distinct styles: camera-ready aspirational and documentary-reminiscent den of vice – ashtrays kicked over on expensive sisal flooring, takeaway cartons sitting in front of designer chairs as if they're matching footstools.

Floppy Fringe Man shares Mr Fahrenheit's dress sense: checked shirt over a white T-shirt, faded jeans. The only difference is in their choice of shoe: Mr Fahrenheit favours a hybrid trainer-clog and Floppy Fringe wears a range of cowboy boots. I spot his rucksack, leaning against tonight's pair. The drugsack, I call it.

'Liking the raincoat,' the frizzy-haired dance teacher says loudly to the room, not looking at me. 'Hood up, drawstrings pulled tight – stylish.' The rest of them laugh.

This is the first time Mr Fahrenheit has sworn at me, the first time his friends have weighed in on his side. I wait for the feelings of humiliation to subside, and tell myself that it doesn't matter what some rude strangers think about my raincoat. I hope I don't cry. When I feel calm enough to speak, I say, 'You can ignore me tonight, Justin, but my problem with your behaviour isn't going to go away. If you won't listen to me, I'll have to find someone who will. Like the police, maybe.'

'Good luck, mate,' says Angie, stressing the last word sarcastically. 'And...dream on. No one's going to stop us listening to a few songs in our own house on a Saturday night.'

'Whose house?' Justin teases her. She pretends to laugh along but I don't think she enjoys the joke as much as he does.

'Louise!' He points at me, arm raised. More of a salute, really. 'I promise you, one day you'll find yourself on the receiving end of the killjoy shit you're so keen on giving out. Yeah! Wherever you're living when your boy's a teenager, unless it's somewhere out in the sticks with no neighbours, some twat's going to bang on your windows when your lad and his pals are letting their hair down and you're going to think, "What a fucking twat, they're just having a laugh." You know what, Louise? You're that twat, right here and now.' He nods as if he's said something profound. 'Oh, wait, sorry – I forgot, your son's already left home, hasn't he? You've sent him away – isn't that right? How old is he, again? Seven? Bet your house is nice and quiet without him. That why you did it? All this choir shit just an excuse, is it? What, did he turn up the theme tune of fuckin' ... *Balamory* a bit too loud one day?'

I am a solid block of shock. I cannot believe my neighbour would say that to me. That he would think it, even when angry. He couldn't have said it if he hadn't first thought it.

He did. Both. Said and thought.

I can't find anything to say in response. It would serve Justin right if I were still standing here this time tomorrow, glued to the ground by his cruel words.

'Leave it, Jub,' Angie warns. She sounds anxious. I wonder if I look alarming: as if I'm considering climbing in through the window – a dripping, hooded black figure – and choking the life out of him. What an appealing idea.

'She sent her seven-year-old son away?' the dance teacher asks. 'What the *fuck*?'

'Would you rather I played *classical* music?' Mr Fahrenheit taunts me. 'Would you still be such a fuckin' killjoy if I played, I don't know . . . Mozart?'

I wonder why he's imitating Hitler, with his finger in a line over his upper lip. Then I realise it's not a moustache; he's pushing his nose up to indicate snobbery.

'Mozart?' Walking Boots laughs. 'Like you've got any.'

'I have, as it goes,' Mr Fahrenheit tells him. 'You've got to have your classical music. Isn't that right, Louise?' To his friends, he says, 'Wanna hear some, you lowbrow wasters?'

No one does. They groan, swear, laugh.

'Looks like it's just you and me, Louise – the cultured ones. Culture vultures.' He leans closer to the rain barrier between us to wink at me.

I can't be here any more. As quickly as I can without slipping, I climb the steps to the street and hurry home, to the riotous applause of Mr Fahrenheit and his friends.

'Stuart. Stuart!' Words alone aren't going to do it. I push his shoulder with the tips of my fingers.

He opens his eyes and stares at me, flat on his back. 'What?'

'Can you hear that? Listen.'

'Louise. It had better be the morning.'

I disagree. Until I have had at least six hours' sleep, it had better not be. I can sleep in later now that I don't have to get Joseph ready for school, which is why I never do. Every morning I switch on at 6.30, exactly the time I used to have to get up; it's my body's daily protest against the absence of my son.

'Sorry. Middle of the night,' I say. I cannot allow myself to define the present moment as morning, even though technically it is. I haven't had my night yet. This is the Noisy Neighbour Paradox: does one say, 'But it's three in the morning!' to impress upon the selfish oaf next door that it's very, very late? 'Four in the morning', 'five in the morning'? At what point does it start to sound as if, actually, busy people are already singing in the shower, pushing the 'on' buttons on their espresso machines, preparing to jog to the office?

Stuart reaches up with both hands for the two

sides of his pillow, left and right of his head, and tries to fold them over his face as if he's packing himself carefully for delivery somewhere. 'Middle of the night,' he says. 'Then I should still be asleep.'

'Can you hear the music?'

'Yes, but it's not going to stop me from sleeping. I've got a wife for that.'

'It's Verdi. Before that we had Bizet, a bit of Puccini.'

The security light on the St John's College flats at the back of us comes on, shines in my face. A car must have driven too close to the building. I lean forward and drag our single bedroom curtain to the right. The curtain is too narrow; we have to choose which side of the window we want to leave exposed: the security light side or the students' bedroom windows side.

'Mr F must have got a "Best of the Classics" CD free with his Saturday paper,' Stuart says, closing his eyes again.

'It's aimed at me,' I tell him. 'A melodic "fuck you". He's bored of attacking me with his music, so now he's doing it with what he thinks of as mine.'

'Isn't that a bit paranoid?'

I could admit that I've been next door, had yet another argument with Mr Fahrenheit, that the subject of classical music came up. That's the context Stuart's missing. If I told him, he would concede that I'm right about the malice in this latest noise-attack, but he would also criticise me – critisult me, Joseph would say; his invented word that he's so proud of, a hybrid of criticise and insult – for going round on my own: a defenceless woman without my husband to protect me. And then I might critisult him back, because I'm exhausted and frustrated and would find it hard to be tactful. I might raise my voice and point out that whenever I suggest we visit Mr Fahrenheit together to lodge our complaint, or that Stuart goes instead of me for a change, he always responds in the same way: 'Come on, Lou, let's not steam in there. Look, we don't want a scene if we can avoid one, do we? He might call it a night soon.'

Call it a night, call it a morning. Call it a party, call it a little get-together.

That's why I go and complain alone. Because my husband always wants to give it more time, to satisfy himself that we're not a pair of troublemaking hotheads.

'I'm going to ring the police,' I say.

'What?' Stuart hauls himself into a sitting position and rubs the inner corners of his eyes with his thumbs, his hands protruding from his face like antlers. 'Lou, put the brakes on a second, please. The police?'

Yes, yes, the police. The Cambridge police. Not the SS, just a nice, polite, helpful PC in uniform, to say something soothing like, 'Can I respectfully ask that you turn the volume down, please, sir?' They're hardly going to storm Mr Fahrenheit's Farrow-&-Ball-reinforced drug den and riddle him with bullets. More's the pity.

'I can't get to sleep with that coming through the wall, Stuart. What else can I do? I've tried talking to him more than a dozen times, and nothing changes. He doesn't even pretend it will! He's proudly, defiantly noisy, except he calls it "not noisy".'

Stuart reaches for the chain on his bedside lamp and pulls. Then, as if the light is an affront to the room full of night that he ought to be sleeping in, he turns it off again. 'Maybe ringing the police is a sensible next step, but not tonight, Lou.'

'When, then?'

'First thing tomorrow?' Stuart says hopefully.

'What, when Mr Fahrenheit's asleep and there's

no music playing?' I assume this will be enough to alert my husband to his temporary lapse into idiocy, but apparently not.

'Yeah. You don't need "Video Killed the Radio Star" pounding out to prove your point. You can explain the situation, the history. It's not as if the police are going to doubt you.'

'Really? You don't think their first thought will be, "Hmm, I wonder if the neighbour's music really *is* too loud or whether this woman is a neurotic spoilsport trying to make sure no one has any fun. If only we could *hear* the music and judge for ourselves – that would be really helpful"?'

'All right, look, I just think…I need to go to sleep, Lou. Imran's coming first thing in the morning. If you can't sleep in here, go up to the attic and sleep on the sofa bed in my study.'

No. No. I want to sleep in my own bed. If I sleep anywhere else, Mr Fahrenheit has won. And I wouldn't be able to fall asleep, anyway; I would lie flat on my back, rigid as a floorboard, with my heart pounding, and the knowledge that I had allowed myself to be driven out of my own bedroom buzzing in my brain like an unswattable fly.

Stuart says, 'If you ring the police now and they

say they'll come out, that means me staying up God knows how long –'

'No, it doesn't,' I say, in what I hope is a calm and helpful voice. I employ the same tactics with my husband as I do with my inconsiderate shit of a next-door neighbour: better not to let them see how angry I am in case they use it against me. 'You can sleep. I'm awake anyway. I'll deal with the police, assuming they can come at such short notice.'

Stuart jolts in the bed, as if I've dropped a hand grenade into his lap. 'I'm not letting you do that on your own,' he says. 'Please, can we just leave it for tonight? I'm knackered, Lou. You must be too.'

Him first, me second. It doesn't mean he's selfish, I tell myself. It's only natural to think of yourself first. We all do it. I'm selfish too. It's lucky no one can read my mind and see the list of things I would allow to happen to Mr Fahrenheit rather than have him disrupt any more of my nights.

Stuart hasn't spotted that my pyjama bottoms are drenched from the knees down. I suppose it must be hard to see a detail like that in the dark. If he notices, he will accuse me of lacking a sense of proportion; he wouldn't willingly get his clothes soaked unless someone's life was at stake and even then it might have to be a blood relative.

'You're right,' I say neutrally. 'I'll go up to the attic. You go back to sleep. Sorry I woke you.'

'Good,' Stuart says with relief. He is so gullible. I love my husband, but there is no doubt that my life flows more easily when I tell him as little as possible. This isn't a new development; I first noticed it shortly after Joseph was born, though I would find it hard to point to any actual secrets I've kept – it's always tiny things I've forgotten by the next day. I have the form of a deceiver without the content.

Stuart makes his 'I'm too tired to say goodnight' noise. I know he'll be unconscious again within seconds, loud Verdi notwithstanding. His talent for sleeping in almost any conditions is the reason he is able to be so sanguine about Mr Fahrenheit's weekend disturbances: his sleep is not threatened, only mine.

'This . . . Imran, tomorrow,' I say. 'Can you . . . delay him?'

'Not really. He's coming at eight-thirty. Realistically, he's going to be here an hour at least, and we have to be at Saviour for ten –'

'No, I mean . . . can you tell him not to come at all? Just . . . I mean, we don't have to rush into it, do we?'

'He's supposed to be starting a week on Monday. What?' Stuart turns on his bedside lamp. 'What does that face mean? Louise, we've been through this.'

'Thirty thousand pounds is a lot of money to spend on a house we might not be staying in, especially when there's no real need.'

'Might not be staying? Since when? Is this about Mr Fahrenheit?'

'I don't want to live next door to him,' I say.

Stuart expresses his displeasure by leaning forward and falling on to his side across the bed. He picks up my pillow and covers his face with it. 'That's the opposite of what you said yesterday. You said, "I'm not being driven out of—"'

'I've changed my mind.'

'Well, look, if you're serious about moving, definitely don't ring the police. You have to declare any official noise disputes with neighbours when you sell a house, or your buyer can sue you.'

I wonder if this means we could sue our vendor. She told us she wanted to move because the house was too big for a woman living alone. I wonder if that was only part of the reason.

'I can't live next door to Justin Clay,' I tell Stuart. 'Even if he never plays a single song ever again, I can't stand being so close to him, not now that I know what he's like. It's like ... living in enemy territory. Seriously, Stuart, can you text Imran now and cancel him?'

If I told him what Justin said about our sending Joseph away in order to have a quieter house, would it make a difference? For the moment, I can't face it. All I want is to push as far away from myself as possible the knowledge that it happened, the memory of it.

'I'm not making any decisions now, Lou, and neither are you. We both need to get some rest. Please?'

Which means he is not going to text Imran and tell him not to come tomorrow. By the time he wakes up it will be too late: Imran will be on his way.

A sharp spurt of disillusionment dulls and solidifies, as they tend to these days, into a small grey stone that rolls slowly down a spiral slide – one that narrows as it descends – until it falls off at the bottom and into the pit of my stomach, and then I don't feel anything any more, once the slight discomfort of the dropping and landing is over.

Obviously I know that there isn't really a spiral slide inside my body, and that a flattened hope cannot transform into a grey pebble. It's funny that sometimes you can only describe something with perfect accuracy by being wildly inaccurate.

'Tomorrow afternoon, soon as we get back, I'll go next door and have a word with Fahrenheit, the ignorant tosser,' Stuart promises. 'I'll tell him, final warning, or we're going to make an official complaint.'

'Why wait till the afternoon?' I ask. 'Why not eight in the morning, before Imran gets here?'

Stuart chuckles. 'Have you ever known Mr F to surface before midday?'

'So . . . you don't want to wake him up?'

He looks caught out. Then he says, 'We might as well give the peace talks a chance, Lou. If we wake him at eight, he won't be amenable to anything we say.'

Cowardice dressed up as strategy. Another little grey pebble loops down the helter-skelter, slowing as it goes, contrary to the laws of whatever the scientific term is for the acceleration of small things rolling downwards.

I pat Stuart's arm. 'Go to sleep,' I say. 'Busy day tomorrow.'

𝄞

The phone rings once before I pounce on it. 'Hello?'

'Mrs Beeston?'

'Yes, it's me.'

'It's Trevor Chibnall, environmental health officer for Cambridge City Council, returning your call.'

'Yes.' Who else would it be at two in the morning? And he isn't returning my call; that makes it sound as if I left a message for him.

'I believe you contacted the police with regard to a noise nuisance issue, and they advised you to contact the council?'

He believes? It's what I told him when we spoke a few minutes ago. I'm tempted to say, 'No, that's completely wrong,' to see if he says, 'But . . . it's what you told me yourself, before.'

'Thanks for ringing me back,' I say instead, though I don't understand why he created the need by ending our first telephone conversation. He didn't explain, just asked for my name and number and said he'd be in touch shortly. I assumed the worst – that he meant days, maybe even weeks – and asked what 'shortly' meant, only to find that my outrage had nowhere to go when he said ten to fifteen minutes.

He is as good as his word, and now I have nowhere to put my unsubstantiated feelings of abandonment. They flap around my heart like empty sacks of flesh after liposuction.

'The number the police gave you is the out-of-hours emergency number. Do you have a noise situation that you'd classify as an emergency?'

I try to focus on Chibnall's question and not his tone, which, in isolation, would be enough to convince me that nothing will happen soon if he has anything to do with it. His voice is deep, serious and devoid of drive. It would be great for telling a coma victim not to resist, to move towards the light.

'It's an emergency in the sense that I'd like something done about it now,' I say. 'I'm still hoping I might get some sleep tonight.' *In my own bed.* 'Can you hear that music?'

'Yes.'

'Loud, isn't it? It's not playing in my house. That's my neighbour.' Knowing nothing about Chibnall's musical preferences, I do not add, *It might be Rachmaninov at the moment but it was Wagner ten minutes ago.*

'Your address, please?'

'Seventeen Weldon Road.'

'Cambridge?'

No, Southampton. That's why I rang Cambridge's environmental health department. 'Yes.'

'Your full name, please?'

I'm not liking the way this is going. His reactions seem off. Or rather, he's not reacting at all, when he ought to be. I was hoping that our dialogue might go as follows:

Loud, isn't it? It's not playing in my house. That's my neighbour.

You're kidding me? Seriously? Wow, that is beyond appalling! There's no way you should have to put up with that at this time of night! Right — sit tight, and I'll come round and sort the bastard out.

What's the point of having an emergency noise officer if tidings of inappropriate noise don't send him over the edge into vengeful hysteria?

'Louise Caroline Beeston,' I tell him.

'And your postcode?'

'CB1 2YL.'

'Your neighbour's full address?'

'Nineteen Weldon Road. Same postcode, I assume.'

'Yes, it is.'

How does he know that? Is he sitting next to a whiteboard covered in photographs of Cambridge's most malevolent noise pests, with the details of each one scrawled in blue wipe-off pen beneath his or her mugshot: the public enemies Chibnall and his team have been hunting for years, but they've never been able to make anything stick?

Either that or I watch too much television.

'And you've lived at number seventeen for how long?' he asks me. No intonation whatsoever.

'Five months.' What does it matter how long I've lived here?

'And your neighbour's been at number nineteen for how long?'

I take a deep breath. Then another. How long is he going to linger over boring, unimportant details? 'Since we moved in. That's all I know.'

'What's your neighbour's full name?'

'His name's Justin Clay. I don't know if he's got a middle name.' Wanting to remind Chibnall that I'm a person and not merely a data source, I say, 'My husband and I call him Mr Fahrenheit. You know, from the Queen song, "Don't Stop Me Now"? He plays it all the time. So . . . please do. Stop him now.' I fake a laugh, then feel like an idiot.

'And Mr Clay has been resident at number nineteen since you moved into number seventeen?' Chibnall asks, his bland manner unaffected by my attempt to make our conversation more interesting.

'Yes.'

'How many people live at number nineteen in total?'

Oh, God, this is unbearable. Is he going to ask me if Mr Fahrenheit has any pets? Is his plan to solve my problem by asking me pointless questions until I die of old age? 'Just him. Though his girlfriend stays a lot.'

'But she isn't a permanent resident of the house?'

'No.'

'Can you describe to me the nature of the problem?' says Chibnall.

'Every second or third Saturday night, he plays loud music that stops me from getting to sleep. I can feel the bass-line pounding in my house.'

'Approximately from what time until what time, or does it vary?'

'Not really. They always go to the pub for a few drinks first, so it tends to start at about ten. And finishes between one and one-thirty. Hello?' I say, when Chibnall doesn't respond.

'It's later than one-thirty now,' he says.

'Yes. This is the latest he's ever gone on, and it's his way of saying "Screw you". I went round about two hours ago and asked him to turn it down. This is my punishment. But even when he's not punishing me, the music is always this loud or louder and it usually has lyrics, and Mr . . . Clay and his friends all yell along to them.' *Drunkenly.* I don't say that, in case I sound prudish. Which I'm not. I have friends who drink far too much and who wouldn't dream of depriving their neighbours of sleep or peace of mind. It's possible to be a considerate alcoholic. 'I mean, that's not okay for him to do that to me, is it? Can you . . . I mean, is there something you can do to stop him? He must be breaking a law – disturbance of the peace, antisocial behaviour –'

'Someone would need to come out to you to assess the situation before offering an opinion.'

'Right.' My rage pulls itself tight inside me. 'So . . . could that person be you, tonight?' I try to disguise my sarcasm as harmless banter, and end up sounding like a grotesque parody of a Hollywood romantic comedy. I grimace at myself in the mirror above the fireplace. My skin looks faded. I have too little colour, while everything else in my lounge has too much: the purple flowers on the curtains seem to throb against the mint green background; the white wall behind me looks almost yellow. It's the light: up too high, parodying daytime. It should have been switched off hours ago. I would turn it down, but I'm too far from the dimmer switch, and there's something grimly satisfying about this ghastly vision of my haggard self: this is what Mr Fahrenheit has done to me.

'If I can fit you in before handover, I'll attend myself,' Trevor Chibnall says. 'If not, it'll be my colleague. I think that's going to be more likely. Either way, someone should be with you within the hour.'

'Oh.' This is unexpected. I run his words through my mind a few times to check I understood them correctly. Yes, it seems so. Apparently something is going to happen. The inert voice misled me; Trevor

Chibnall is about to spring into action. I hope it's the action of sending his colleague rather than himself. I am willing to wait longer if I can have someone who knows how to put expression into his or her voice. 'Great,' I say.

'Thank you for your call.'

'Wait, I... if you send someone out to me, is that an official thing?' I ask. 'I mean, does it get... recorded somewhere, formally? My husband thinks we might have trouble selling the house if we register a noise problem and then –'

'No, nothing becomes official in that sense simply by our coming out to you.'

'Not that we *want* to move, and hopefully we won't have to, but –'

'It's not helpful to us when people spread scare stories about it being impossible to sell houses because of a noise dispute with a neighbour,' he says. 'If we find that there's a noise nuisance, we take steps to remedy the situation.'

From someone more imaginative, this might be a euphemism for slicing Mr Fahrenheit's head clean off his neck. Not from Chibnall, I don't think. I picture him thinking inertly about the filling in of forms, looking as washed-out under the glare

SOPHIE HANNAH

of the neon lights in his office as I look in my lounge mirror. I can't assemble a face for him in my imagination: a featureless taupe blur is the best I can do.

'Once it's remedied, there's no reason why someone wouldn't buy a house that formerly had a noise problem,' he drones on. 'But we can't find evidence of a noise nuisance and set about rectifying it if people don't report these things because they've heard from a friend or a colleague that they reported a similar problem and were then obliged to declare it and couldn't sell their house.'

'I agree,' I tell him. Though in theory I'm happy to gang up with the council's environmental health officer against my husband, I'm slightly concerned that he seems more exercised about scaremongering in relation to the sale of houses than about Mr Fahrenheit's behaviour. 'That's why I'm reporting it, and very much looking forward to your rectification.'

'An environmental health officer will be with you shortly, Mrs Beeston,' says Chibnall.

'Thank you.'

The line goes dead. I put the phone back on its base, go to the kitchen where Mr Fahrenheit's

music is slightly less audible, fill the kettle with
water and switch it on. I need strong tea. It's past
two in the morning, I'm exhausted, and I'm about
to have what I can only think of as a very important
meeting.

I wonder if I need to prepare in any way. Nothing
about the house needs sorting out; everything is
in order and ready to give a good impression: no
empty wine bottles on their sides, no upturned
ashtrays.

No evidence that a child lives here. All Joseph's
toys are tidily packed away in his room, as they have
been since the beginning of term.

I drum the palms of my hands on the kitchen
countertop while I wait for the kettle to boil. Will
Chibnall, or his colleague, need to inspect the
whole house, every floor? What if he asks me why
there's a room that clearly belongs to a child but
is empty? He's bound to be thorough, to want to
see how far the noise from Mr Fahrenheit's stereo
travels, but maybe if I close Joseph's door then he
won't go in there.

I have a better idea: if I close Joseph's door, I
can tell Chibnall that Joseph is in there, asleep.
Yes, it's a lie, but a harmless one. I might not even

need to tell him explicitly. There's a sign Blu-tacked to the door saying 'Joseph's Room', each shaky capital letter a different colour. If Chibnall sees that on a closed door, he will assume that there's a sleeping child behind it, and won't ask to be let in. Anyone would make that assumption. Where else would a seven-year-old boy be in the early hours of a Sunday morning but at home, safely tucked up in his bed?

Stop it. Don't think it.

Safe in his bed, with his mum and dad just along the hall in case he needs anything in the night, in case he has a bad dream and needs a cuddle . . .

I bend over, gasp for breath. Why do I do this to myself? It might not be so bad if I didn't fill my mind with the very words that will hurt me the most. There's another way of defining Joseph's absence, one that's nowhere near as painful. Other words to describe the situation, which is, in so many ways, a good and fortunate situation – so why do I never use them?

The sound of the kettle clicking off snaps me back to sanity. I move towards it, put my face near the steam; close enough to feel its wet warmth without risking a burn.

Was I really, only a few seconds ago, planning to deceive the council's emergency noise person about the whereabouts of my son? Crazy. I mustn't do it. It would imply guilt that, according to Stuart, I have no need to feel. We have done nothing wrong: the opposite. We'd be harming Joseph by keeping him at home, harming his future. I will tell Chibnall the truth, and, if he looks disapproving, I will pretend to be Stuart and say all the things he says to me several times a day.

Warning myself that I shouldn't – silently insisting that I won't and am not – I open the drawer where I keep tea towels. I lift them all out and take out the small plastic pouch full of cannabis that I stole from Mr Fahrenheit's house a few weeks ago when I went round to complain. We were standing in his kitchen, which has a large granite-topped island at its centre – extra drug preparation space – and shiny silver pans hanging down from the ceiling above it like a contemporary art chandelier. Mr Fahrenheit got angry with me and left the room, and I picked up one of the three little bags of marijuana from the island and slipped it into my jeans pocket.

I wonder what effect it would have on me.

Would I relax so much that I wouldn't care about anything any more? I haven't got any cigarettes or Rizlas in the house, so I can't roll a joint, but I've watched Mr Fahrenheit do it another way: with a plastic bottle, a hole burned out of its bottom. The bottle fills up with smoke at a certain point, I think, but I'm not sure how or if there's any other equipment involved – I only saw Mr Fahrenheit do it once, when I was walking past his house and he'd forgotten to close the curtains. He was on his own in his lounge. He takes drugs in every part of his house, every day, Stuart and I have worked out, but only ever listens to music in the basement.

Sighing, because I would try some if it were easier but it isn't, I put the little plastic bag back in the drawer and cover it with the tea towels. I probably ought to throw it away in case Trevor Chibnall stumbles upon it, but I don't want to. And he's unlikely to root around in my kitchen drawers. How ridiculous that I'm worried about him discovering my son's absence but not my stash of illegal drugs.

I stir two sugars into my milky tea, although I don't normally take sugar. It will give me some energy.

The Rachmaninov stops. I wonder what Mr Fahrenheit will play next. He must be sick of classical music by now.

Come on, Mr F. Put something on, anything. Something really crass and intrusive that will prove my point, so that I won't need to say anything at all when Chibnall arrives.

My doorbell rings.

'It stopped a few seconds before you rang the bell, literally,' I tell Patricia Jervis, the Trevor Chibnall substitute who is sitting on my sofa, holding the mug of Earl Grey I made her in one hand and a pen in the other. She is short and stocky – in her late fifties, I'd guess – with curly grey hair held back from her make-up-free face by a green sweatband that is consistent with the rest of her PE teacher look: navy blue tracksuit, ribbed white socks, blue-and-grey trainers. I have been told to call her Pat because everyone else does, though she sounded far from happy about everyone else doing so when she said it. She's writing in a notebook that is balanced on her lap. 'Are you parked right outside?' I ask her.

'Hmm?' she says without looking up. 'Yes. Yes, I am.'

Five seconds to lock her car and check it's locked, another seven to walk to my front door...I know from my own experience that whenever Mr Fahrenheit's music is audible in my house, it's also audible from the street. 'Didn't you hear anything when you first got out of the car?' I ask. 'Classical music. It was loud. You must have heard it.'

Pat Jervis smiles down at her notebook. 'There's nothing wrong with my hearing,' she says, dodging the question. 'We all have to take hearing tests regularly. If you're worried that I don't believe you, don't be. Our department handles upwards of two hundred noise disputes a year. Would you care to guess in how many of those cases the complainant turns out not to have a valid objection?'

I shake my head.

'This year so far, none. Last year there was one. People don't sit up all night chatting to environmental health officers because they like the attention. It tends to be a desperate last resort.'

'Yes.' She wouldn't like it if I threw myself at her feet and said, 'Thank you for understanding.'

Does everyone do that as well as calling her Pat? Has anyone ever done it?

'Seems to be an unfortunate fact of life that those adversely affected by noise nuisance are often so doubtful they'll be believed and so reluctant to cause trouble that they suffer in silence for years.'

'Or suffer in noise,' I quip.

'Yes, they suffer in noise for years.' She repeats my silly joke, straight-faced, then smiles at her notebook again. 'Meanwhile, the antisocial neighbours responsible for the anguish and disruption tend to have no such confidence problems,' she says. 'No doubts about their rights and righteousness whatsoever. They're convinced that any official procedure will find in their favour, and couldn't be more astonished when we tell them we're going to be taking legal action against them if they don't adjust their behaviour.'

Anguish. Legal action. These are all good words. I prefer Pat Jervis to Trevor Chibnall. I prefer her vocabulary. She bends forward to rub her ankle with her left hand. I noticed as she wandered around my kitchen looking at the seascapes on the wall that she rocks slightly to the left and right as she walks. 'You like paintings of the sea, then,' she said, touching the glass of one frame with the tip of her index finger. I told her the sea was only in the kitchen; none of the other rooms have themed art. I am averse to themed anything, generally, and have no idea why I decided to fill the walls of one particular room of my house with pictures of boats, sandy beaches, waves against distant horizons; I told Pat Jervis that too. 'Very interesting,' she said, sounding as if she meant it, but, at the same time, wanted to draw a line under the subject.

I am working on a theory that people employed by the council are not the same as the rest of us. It's still in the early stages of development.

Pat asks me all the same questions that Trevor Chibnall asked and more. She writes down my answers. I notice that her hands look older than the rest of her – the skin dry and creased like paper – and decide that it would make a good horror story: a woman whose job it is to transcribe – day after day, night after night – the details of other people's suffering, and whose hands age prematurely as a result.

Her voice is friendly enough, though making eye contact seems to be a problem for her. Does each member of the environmental health department have a different strength that compensates for another team member's weakness? Maybe Chibnall, if he were here, would give me the most amazing, sympathetic, bonding looks to offset his monotone and I would end up liking him better.

'Any children live in the house with you?' Pat asks.

I pull myself up straight. 'Yes, but . . . not at the moment.'

'That's fine.' She writes on her pad. 'Joint custody situation? Child from a previous marriage?'

'No, I . . .' It's not fine. It's not fine at all. 'My son Joseph lives here during the school holidays. He's seven.'

'But he lives here at least some of the time?' Pat asks.

Did she notice how terrible that sounded? How bad a mother it made me sound? If her manner were less straightforward I would suspect her of snideness, of deliberately crafting a double-edged comment that I can't prove she meant in the worst way.

'Just that it's useful in a noise case if we can say a child lives in the affected house. Homework, good night's sleep, all that stuff. We trot it all out.' Pat chuckles into her tea. 'Ironic, since children are far less bothered by noise disturbances than adults, as a rule, but there you go.'

Did she say 'the afflicted house'? No. 'Affected', it must have been.

Stuart and I don't have to worry about Joseph's homework, and neither does Pat Jervis; the doing of it will never take place at home. This has been put to me as one of the great advantages of the status quo. When our family is reassembled, in the school holidays, we can relax and have fun together, and Stuart and I will never have to harangue Joseph about learning his times tables, as the parents of day-schoolers have to.

'All right,' says Pat, looking down at her notes. 'So you've attempted to discuss the situation with Mr Clay on numerous occasions, and he's been consistently unsympathetic to your predicament – would you say that's an accurate description of what's occurred?'

'Yes.'

'Yes,' Pat repeats.

'Until tonight, what's always happened is that he's argued with me, then reluctantly agreed to turn it down a bit, but he's always turned it back up by the time I've got back home and taken off my coat.'

'Doesn't surprise me at all,' says Pat. 'It's a classic tactic. He's banking on you being too embarrassed or tired to go back a second time in one night. Have you ever?'

'No.'

'No,' she echoes me again. 'If you did, do you know what he'd say? "I turned it down. You asked me to turn it down and I did." And he'd think he was clever for saying it. Now, is there anything I haven't asked or you haven't told me that you think I need to know?'

'Nothing that has anything to do with the noise issue specifically,' I say.

'Spit it out,' Pat says briskly.

'Just … about my son not being here. Justin Clay's probably going to tell you that I sent my son away because he made too much noise in the house, and that's just rubbish. It's a lie.'

Pat looks up at me. Finally. 'You'd better tell me the situation with your son,' she says.

'He's a pupil at Saviour College School, a boarder. He has to be – they won't let you be in the choir and live at home. Yeah.' I nod, seeing Pat raise her eyebrows. 'They're the great Saviour

47

College and they know best about everything. My son's a junior probationer in the boys' choir, which is the absolute elite of the school – oh, it's all so ridiculous to anyone outside Saviour's stupid, closeted, music-obsessed little ... bubble! I mean, does it make sense to you? A school with four hundred-odd pupils, three hundred and eighty-four of whom have a choice of whether to board or not, or they can board during the week and go home at weekends, and then there are the sixteen choirboys who are forcibly separated from their families for the whole of each term, no matter what those families happen to think about it. It's like some kind of ... awful primitive sacrifice!'

'Mrs Beeston ...' Pat Jervis leans forward.

'You can call me Louise.'

'Louise. I don't mean to sound uncaring, but ... how does this relate to the dispute between yourself and Mr Clay? This is about his antisocial behaviour, not your family's educational choices.'

'Yes.'

Except I don't have a choice. Dr Ivan Freeman, director of music at Saviour, believes that Joseph, as one of his precious choir's probationers, belongs to him at least as much as he belongs to me and Stuart. In Dr

Freeman's eyes, we have as little right to comment as Mr Fahrenheit has in mine.

'I know a bit about Saviour College,' Pat says. 'Friend of mine's a bed-maker there, took me to see the boys' choir once, in the chapel. They were brilliant. I say go for it, much as you'd rather have your son here – I appreciate that, but it's an amazing opportunity for him. My friend says Saviour's choristers have gone on to have amazing musical careers, some of them – famous opera singers, prize-winning classical composers, all sorts. Real star stuff, she says. If your boy does well in that choir, he'll be set up for life. And don't they waive the fees for choirboys? You can't say no to a deal like that, can you?'

'On the noise nuisance front, what's the next step?' I ask abruptly. Pat's speech about the benefits of a Saviour chorister education is uncannily similar to the one Dr Freeman regularly delivers. I've also heard versions of it from several of the other choirboys' parents. I suppose they have to try and believe it's worth it.

'Next step.' Pat slaps her notebook closed, making me jump. 'If you're happy to make it official, I can arrange to have a communication sent out to Mr

Clay on Monday morning, first class post, so he'll get it Tuesday. At first all we do is notify him that a complaint's been made, what might happen down the line –'

'Which is what?'

'Well, we'll inform him that we'll be monitoring the situation,' says Pat.

Monitoring. That sounds like a terrifying disincentive.

'Any instances of unwelcome noise in the future, you call us out straight away, we assess the disturbance. If we agree it's a problem, we speak to Mr Clay in person, give him a final chance to behave reasonably. If he persists with the nuisance, we serve him with a noise abatement order.'

I try to listen to her, but the paranoid babble in my head is drowning out her voice. What if he does what he did tonight every time: turns off the music when he sees her car pull up outside my house so that she never catches him, never has a chance to assess his noise and label it problematic?

I'm so tired; my brain feels like a swollen balloon that's about to burst.

'After that, assuming he violates the order, we're into serious measures,' Pat is saying. 'Confiscating his music equipment — speakers, sound system. Sometimes it goes as far as a court case. People are fined, some spend time behind bars.'

A custodial sentence for playing Queen at too high a volume? 'Really?' I say.

'I've known noise pests to be that stubborn, yes.'

I picture Mr Fahrenheit in the dock, facing a stretch in solitary confinement. I kind of hope it goes as far as a trial at least, though I wouldn't honestly want him to be locked up: that would be excessive. I am feeling more lenient, now that Pat has convinced me she can solve my problem.

I realise that until she does, I can't put the house up for sale. Legal obligations notwithstanding, I couldn't live with myself if I sold it with an untamed Mr Fahrenheit next door. No, there's a better way: Pat will sort everything out, and then I'll be able to tell our buyer the full story, complete with happy ending. And give them Pat's phone number, just in case Mr Fahrenheit tries his luck again once I'm gone.

'Nine cases out of ten, the first letter we send out does the trick,' Pat says. 'Oh, it'd be very useful if you could log all incidents, keep a noise diary — also, of any interactions between you and your

SOPHIE HANNAH

neighbour, your husband and your neighbour, even your son, though obviously he's not here at the moment. But when he is. Anything at all. There's no knowing at this point what we're going to need, so, if in doubt, put it in the log. Depending on how stubborn your neighbour is and how much he wants a fight, it might come in useful.'

'All right,' I say. 'Should I log what happened tonight?'

'Yes, might as well.' Pat stands up. 'And remember, next time it happens, ring me straight away. Me or Trevor or Doug. You've got all the numbers, have you? Office hours, emergency call-out?'

'Yes, thank you.'

Pat walks up to the mirror and touches its surface with the index finger of her right hand, exactly as she did with the glass of the framed painting in the kitchen. What an odd woman she is. Still, she's also the noise nuisance Terminator, so she can do no wrong as far as I'm concerned.

Once she's had enough of pressing my mirror with her fingertip, she turns to face me and stares past my right shoulder into mid-air, as if that's where I'm standing. 'People whine that there's no point ringing the council, they never do anything,' she says. 'Nothing could be further from the truth. You watch – you'll see. We'll sort out your Mr Clay. I don't see it taking very long.'

I feel less reassured than I did a few seconds ago. Is she allowed to be so cocky? Doesn't the same council rule book that forbids eye contact in case a member of the public misinterprets it and falls in love with you also warn against promising people favourable outcomes that you can't possibly guarantee?

'I'm not allowed to tell you that officially.' Pat plays with the zip on her tracksuit top, pulling it up and down. 'Trevor wouldn't. Doug wouldn't. Never get their hopes up, that's what we're told, but I say if it goes our way, there's no harm in having started celebrating early, and if it doesn't go our way, well . . .' She spreads her arms as if it's obvious. 'You're not going to feel any worse because you spent a few months hoping for the best, are you? I've yet to meet someone things have gone wrong for who wishes they'd started feeling miserable a damn sight sooner. Have you?'

'No. But . . .'

'Goodnight, Mrs Beeston. Louise, sorry.' Pat shakes my hand without looking at me. 'Get some sleep. But fill in the log for tonight first, if you would. You'd be amazed how much detail a night's sleep can wipe out.'

I open the front door for her and she hurries away, bobbing from left to right as she goes.

𝄞

I sit up, my eyes still glued together with sleep. My mind slumps forward inside my body: boneless grey mush that I must force into an upright position because something is happening and it's frightening, and I need to think about what it means.

Music. Different. Too close.

I open my eyes and feel as if I'm breaking them. Something's not right. I run my fingertips along the hollows beneath them. They don't feel hollow. They stick out: lumpy. It's as if they've been filled in with a thick substance that has swollen and started to rot. Perhaps it's just tiredness, or a build-up of angry tears I've held back. Moving my eyelids is like driving two sharp pins into the back of my skull.

What time is it? I could find out by reaching for my phone on the bedside table.

The singing isn't coming from next door's basement this time. It can't be. This is sound that has travelled no distance. Children's voices. Boys.

Stuart snores beside me: a different rhythm from the music playing on the other side of the wall. That's where it must be coming from: Mr Fahrenheit's bedroom.

That's Joseph singing.

No.

The tune isn't one I've heard, but I know the words very well. It's the Opening Responses. Saviour College's chaplain and the boys' choir sing them at the beginning of every Choral Evensong.

O Lord, open thou our lips:
And our mouth shall shew forth thy praise.

O God, make speed to save us:
O Lord, make haste to help us.

Glory be to the Father, and to the Son, and to the Holy Ghost.
As it was in the beginning, is now, and ever shall be, world without end. Amen.

Praise ye the Lord.
The Lord's name be praised.

There are many different musical settings for these words, just as there are for what Joseph calls the 'Mag' and the 'Nunc': the Magnificat and the Nunc Dimittis. Before Saviour College School kidnapped my son, he didn't know the street names of any liturgical pieces of music.

That's Joseph singing.

No. Impossible.

I can hear my son singing to me through the bedroom wall.

I am shaking. Trying very hard not to scream. I think I'm about to fail.

𝄞

Noise Diary – Sunday 30 September, 5.25 a.m.

I have just put the phone down after having had the following conversation with Doug Minns from Cambridge City Council's environmental health team. What follows is pretty much word for word, I think.

Me: Hello, could I speak to Pat Jervis, please?

Him: Can I ask what it's in connection with?

Me: A noise problem. My name's Louise Beeston.
      I live at 17 Weldon Road—

Him: Your details are in front of me. Mrs Louise
      Beeston. Noise disturbance from a
      neighbour at number 19. Loud music.

Me: Yes, that's right. If Pat's still on duty, I'd
      really like her to come out to me again
      and—

Him: You first rang this number to report a noise
      nuisance at 1.45 a.m. Is that correct?

Me: I don't know. Yes, probably. It was around
      that time. But since then—

Him: Is the noise still continuing at an
      unacceptable level?

Me: If you'd listen to what I'm trying to tell you,

you might know the answer to that by now.
Will you please let me speak?

Him: I'm trying to establish the current situation,
      Mrs Beeston. Is the noise nuisance ongoing?

Me: He's not making a noise now this second,
      but he just woke me up, only about half an
      hour after I'd fallen asleep. Deliberately. I'd
      like Pat to come and—

Him: It's not possible for anybody to come out
      to you if there's no noise being made at
      present. First thing on Monday, I can send
      a communication to your neighbour to the
      effect that there's been a noise complaint
      made against him. Also, if you could log—

Me: You don't understand. Yes, I'll log everything
      and yes, please, send him a letter, but I
      need someone to put the fear of God into
      him now, tonight. Otherwise what's to stop
      him waking me up again in another hour, even
      assuming I could fall asleep? This is more
      than noise nuisance – it's deliberate torture.

Him: This is our only emergency line, Mrs Beeston. I'm on duty as the emergency officer. At present there's nobody in the office aside from myself. I can't stay on this line talking to you once I've established that you're not suffering an ongoing noise nuisance that needs urgent attention.

Me: If you'd bloody well listen to me, you'd find out that it *is* ongoing. He was playing music before, loudly – ask Trevor Chibnall. He heard it, when I rang him at 1.45. Then he stopped when—

Him: 'Ongoing' means that the music is playing now. Is it?

Me: No. I've said that. But—

Him: Then I'll have to ask you to ring again on Monday morning. I'm sorry, Mrs Beeston, but that's our policy.

Me: You are the least helpful human being I've ever had the misfortune to speak to. Goodbye.

So, as I hope the above script demonstrates, I was not allowed to explain the situation. I will attempt to do so here, where there is no danger of my clogging up an important phone line.

At 2 a.m., when I rang the council's out-of-hours noise number for the first time, my neighbour at number 19 Weldon Road, Justin Clay, was playing loud music which Trevor Chibnall heard. Mr Clay had been playing loud music continuously since shortly after 10 p.m. What I did not tell Trevor Chibnall was that at first he was playing pop and rock music as he always does, but that after I went round to complain and ask him to turn it down (during which conversation he accused me of being a music snob who only likes classical) he turned off the pop and put on loud classical music instead. I cannot see any way to read this apart from as a deliberate taunt.

Pat Jervis then came out to my house to assess the situation, but by the time she arrived the music had stopped. I worked out that she must have parked outside my house at the exact moment that Mr Clay turned off his music, and I believe he timed this deliberately, to make it look as if I had exaggerated, imagined or spitefully invented the problem.

After Pat Jervis left, I went to bed and took a while to fall asleep because I was so upset and agitated. I finally fell asleep and was then woken again at 4.20 a.m. by more music, again coming from Mr Clay's house, except that this time it wasn't coming from his basement but from his bedroom. Previously, he has always confined his musical activities to the basement. His bedroom is right next to mine (our two houses are mirror images of each other), separated only by an inadequately insulated Victorian wall, and he knows this. When he and I first met, shortly after my family and I moved in next door to him and before there was any problem between us, we looked round each other's houses at his instigation. I thought it was an odd thing for him to suggest, since we didn't know one another, but it soon became obvious that he wanted to show off his no-expense-spared interior. So I hope I've proved that he knows very well where his bedroom is in relation to mine.

The music he was playing in his bedroom was choral music. Specifically, it was a boys' choir, singing liturgical responses of the exact sort that my son sings every Tuesday and Thursday evening at Choral Evensong in Saviour College's chapel: another deliberate taunt. Mr Clay played the responses over and over again – I don't know exactly how many times because I became too upset to count. How loud was it? I suppose these things are relative. My husband, woken by my distress rather than the music, said that it was barely audible. Yet it was loud enough to wake me.

I believe that Mr Clay waited until he saw Pat Jervis leave my house, allowed me just enough time to calm down and fall asleep, and then deliberately woke me up, using a piece of music that he'd specially selected in order to provoke me. What has happened to me tonight is far more serious than a simple noise nuisance. It started as that, but has turned into something vicious and menacing that an unimaginative man like Doug Minns has no predetermined procedure for. Although there is currently no music spilling from my neighbour's house into mine, the problem is

ongoing in the sense that there is basically zero
chance of me getting any more sleep tonight. I'm
too scared of being woken again, which is precisely
the effect Mr Clay must have wanted to achieve.
Given his malicious and calculating track record,
he might well decide to turn the music back on
in another half-hour, and if he doesn't it will be
because he knows he doesn't need to – he knows
he's instilled enough fear and dread in me that I
won't risk closing my eyes. So, yes, the problem
is very much ongoing, because I'm terrified that
he will do this again – maybe not every night but
as often as he feels like it. He can do it any time
he wants, and stop whenever he sees a council
officer's car pull up outside my house, so that
no one ever hears or witnesses anything. And he
knows I know that.

Look, I'm not a fool. I get it. Obviously emergency
out-of-hours noise officers can't waste their time
rushing to houses where once, long ago, there
was a noise somewhere in the vicinity – that would
be ludicrous. I understand why you lot have the
rules you have, but would it kill you to be a bit
flexible? Actually, I'm sure if Pat Jervis had picked

up the phone instead of Doug Minns, the response would have been quite different. Pat seems to be properly on my side. I'm sure she'd have bent the stupid rules, come round, knocked on my neighbour's door and told him in no uncertain terms, 'Cut it out right now, or you could end up in court. This is harassment.'

Maybe I ought to try the police again and tell them that the council's environmental health department has no interest in preventing a gruesome murder on Weldon Road. That would get their attention.

2

I open my eyes and see wooden slats above me. That's right: I lay down on the bottom bunk of Joseph's bed at about 6 a.m., not for a moment imagining that I might fall asleep. That I did feels like a victory, briefly. Then my triumph gives way to disappointment that I didn't manage to sleep for longer. I feel worse than I did before: as if someone's scraped the insides of my eyelids and scrubbed at my brain with a pumice stone.

What time is it? It's fully light outside, and no darker in here. The curtains in Joseph's room are useless: white and gauzy, thin as tissue paper. I've been meaning to replace them since we bought the house and not getting round to it. Joseph, thankfully, cares no more about daylight seeping in than he minds about the noise Mr Fahrenheit makes every other Saturday night. He's completely unaware of both. I'm lucky. Or I used to think I was, until he left home.

Don't say 'left home'. He still lives here. You know that.

Joseph has always been a brilliant sleeper: 7.30 p.m. until 7 a.m., however light, dark, loud or quiet his surroundings. Other mothers think I'm lying when I say this but it's true: he has slept all night every night since he was four weeks old. Even his rare sick spells have always involved the kind of illnesses that have made him need to sleep overtime and more heavily. I used to feel sorry for my friends who had it harder – Eniola, who went three nights without sleep when Matthew had terrible colic, and Jenny, with her frequent dashes to A&E on account of Chloe's asthma.

I envy them now, both of them, and not only them. I envy any parent whose child hasn't been stolen by a school for no good reason, which, come to think of it, is nearly every parent I know – any mother whose son is too insecure and clingy to settle or be happy away from home. It's my fault that

Joseph is as relaxed and independent-minded as he is. As a new parent, I wasn't anxious or neurotic. I regularly left him with babysitters; I believed there was a strong chance they'd be at least as good at looking after a baby as I was, if not better.

If I'd foreseen a conspiracy to take my son away from me, I'd have made sure to be one of those mums who never lets her child out of her sight. I'd have done everything I could to turn Joseph into the sort of boy who believes something bad will happen to him if his mother's not there to protect him.

If I were less tired, I might put the counter-arguments to myself. I would challenge my shameful retrospective plotting, my hyperbolic use of certain words – 'conspiracy', 'stolen', 'fault' – but at the moment I have neither the energy nor the inclination.

I hear Stuart's voice say, 'I thought you were going to sleep in the study,' and realise I'm not alone in the room. I throw back the duvet, trying not to notice the small blue and red sailing boats on its cover. Joseph chose it himself. He ought to be the one throwing it back this morning, not me.

A cross-section of my husband appears in front

of me, blocking out some of the light: part of his legs, his waist and chest. The top bunk blocks his face from my view, but I can imagine what it looks like when he says, 'You'd better get up. Imran'll be here in fifteen minutes. And remember, soon as he leaves we'll have to set off to Saviour, so you need to get properly dressed now.'

I spring up off the bed and am on my feet before he gets to the door. 'I'm sorry?' I say belligerently. 'Since when do you tell me when and how to dress?'

He looks surprised by the strength of my reaction, and I feel guilty. 'You've just woken up, so I thought I'd ... you know.'

He's right. I have just woken up, less than two hours after falling asleep for the second time. Why would I do something so foolish? I wouldn't – not of my own accord. I would do the sensible thing and stay asleep until quarter to ten, which would still give me enough time to leap into the shower before setting off to Saviour College's chapel for Joseph's gig. That's how I irreverently think of the services.

'Did you wake me up?' I ask Stuart.

'Yes. Eventually. It wasn't easy.'

'Thanks a lot. You know what time I got to sleep? Probably about ten past six.'

'Well, I know it was after five-twenty-five a.m.,' Stuart says irritably. 'What should I have done, Lou? Imran's coming all the way from Stamford and he'll be here in—'

'I don't give a fuck about Imran at this precise moment, Stuart! He's not a visiting dignitary that I need to impress, he's one of my oldest friends. You could have said, "Sorry, Imran, Lou's asleep – she's had a hellish night and I didn't want to wake her." He'd have been totally fine about it.'

'Right.' Stuart raises his eyebrows. He takes an unsteady step back, as if an unpredictable wind has knocked him off balance. 'Sorry, I assumed that since we're going to be talking about the work to the house, you might want to be there.'

'Why? You're not going to listen to what I say anyway. You didn't last night, when I asked you to text Imran and put him off. I don't *want* the house sandblasted! The last thing on my mind at the moment is the colour of the brickwork...'

'And yet you're saying I should have left you to sleep and given Imran the go-ahead without you,' Stuart points out with infuriating patience. 'It sounds like you, me and Imran all need to be there, since we're likely to have different opinions. Mine's certainly different from yours.'

He tries again to leave the room. 'Wait,' I say. 'How do you know I didn't get to sleep till after twenty-five past five?' As I ask, I realise that there can only be one answer.

'I found your noise diary,' says Stuart accusingly.

And nothing else? I really ought to hide the drugs I stole from Mr Fahrenheit's place somewhere cleverer. It's not inconceivable that one day Stuart might decide the tea towel currently in use needs washing; it's unlikely, but just about possible, that instead of taking a clean one from the top of the pile in the drawer, he might take the whole lot out and have a look at them all. If he did that, he would spot the small plastic bag full of marijuana underneath and subject me to a horrified interrogation.

'Obviously you were busy last night after I went back to sleep,' he says. 'Much as I'm keen to hear all about what you got up to, we don't have time. Seriously, Lou, since you *are* now awake and Imran's going to be here any minute—'

'I rang the council, not the police,' I say. Then, with heavy sarcasm, 'I didn't disobey you, Master, if that's what you're annoyed about.' It isn't true – I called the police first – but Stuart doesn't need to know that. I don't believe that all is fair in love or in war, but I am coming to believe that all might be fair in marriage, which is a combination of the two.

'I thought I made it pretty clear that I didn't want you ringing anyone,' says Stuart. 'But you did, so there's no point discussing it, is there? Though I have to say, if someone told you to keep a noise diary, I'm sure that...thing on the kitchen table isn't what they had in mind.'

'I was told to keep a record,' I say as neutrally as possible. 'I'm keeping a record.'

'Yeah, well, it reads like the obsessive ramblings of a sleep-deprived neurotic. And while we're on the subject, since you evidently don't care about being ready when Imran arrives...would you mind sleeping on the sofa bed in the attic instead of in Joseph's bed if you can't sleep in our room? As I suggested last night.' Stuart sighs as if there's no point trying to reason with me. 'Remember? I said why don't you make up the sofa bed in my study?'

While we're on the subject? We weren't. Where I ended up sleeping last night has nothing to do with what I wrote in my noise diary. I am baffled by this until

I realise what Stuart must mean. His 'subject' is neither of those things, though both are instances of it. I wonder how he'd define it if I asked him: my dubious behaviour? My insistence on acting in accordance with my own ideas rather than his?

'Don't make out this is *that*, Stuart, okay?'

Stupid. I should have phrased it differently. There is no 'that'. 'That' is something Stuart believes in that doesn't exist. It's one of the more distasteful strands of his campaign to prove that his specialist subject, 'Isn't Louise Mental, Folks?', deserves a place on our core curriculum.

'Three things,' I say. My voice is an ice sculpture. 'One: at six in the morning, on no sleep, why would I choose to make up a sofa bed when there's an already-made bed in here, nearer and warmer than the attic? Two: I didn't sleep in Joseph's bed. He always sleeps in the top bunk. I slept in the bottom bunk, where he never sleeps, and there's *absolutely* nothing wrong with me sleeping there if I want to. Three: all this is irrelevant in this instance because I didn't plan to fall asleep in Joseph's room or anywhere. I'm amazed I was able to after all that stress. I only lay down because I was too knackered to stand up—'

'In Joseph's room, which you haunt like a fucking—' Having cut me off mid-sentence, Stuart does the same to himself. He turns away and stands still with his back to me, as if we're playing 'What's the Time, Mr Wolf?' and he's counting.

'Haunt?' I say.

'That was the wrong word. You know why?' Angry Mr Wolf turns round. 'Because no one's dead! You're not dead, Joseph's not dead, I'm not dead! We're among the most fortunate people on the planet, in fact. So why do I keep finding you in here, moping around your son's ever-so-tidy room as if you're ... mourning him or something? It's creepy, Louise. Can't you see that?'

The doorbell rings.

'And now there's Imran,' Stuart snaps, though the emotional charge of his words is *And now look what you've done*. Even though I never wanted Imran to come round this morning and asked for him to be put off.

Your son's ever-so-tidy room ...

Most people would zoom in on the references to death and mourning, which I agree were pretty unforgivable, but the 'ever-so-tidy' was worse. Subtler, but more potent if you take the time to unpack it.

'This feels a bit like a witch-hunt,' I say calmly, thinking that the defendant always dresses presentably for a court appearance, and this is my feelings doing the same. 'I'm not mourning Joseph in this room or any other because, as you point out, he's very much alive. There's another word that begins with an "m" that fits much better – missing. I'm *missing* my son, who's only seven and who isn't here. Is that all right with you?'

Stuart walks over to the sash window and opens it. 'We'll have to talk about this later. Imran!' he shouts down to the street. 'Hang on. I'm just coming down.'

I consider tearing out two smallish clumps of my hair, to demonstrate my frustration. In my current mood and predicament, hair doesn't feel like something I need each individual strand of. I'd still have plenty left after my grand gesture. 'Don't ever talk about death and mourning in connection with Joseph, ever again,' I say. 'And don't say that his room is ever-so-tidy, because that's a death reference too. Don't . . . yes, it is!' I'm not interested in hearing him deny it. Tears sting the insides of my eyelids, bitter, like a wash of acid. 'Joseph's bedroom is tidy because, since he's not here at the moment, he hasn't had a chance to mess it up since I last tidied it. It's a tidy room – that's all it is! Call it that!'

Stuart is thinking only of Imran: closing the window so that he doesn't overhear.

'Lou, you're massively overreacting to something completely innocuous. I—'

'It wasn't innocuous! "Ever-so-tidy" – I know what that means! Parents whose children die and they meticulously keep the room exactly as it was while they were alive. Like a shrine!'

'I didn't mean that at all.'

'Don't lie to me!' I yell in his face. 'If you didn't mean that, why didn't you just say "tidy"? Why the "ever-so"? Well? You've got no answer, have you? Because I'm right – you were trying to make the point that Joseph's room's *too* tidy, like some kind of ... museum-preserved bedroom of a dead boy!'

Stuart flinches. He backs away from me. 'I'm going downstairs to talk to Imran,' he says. 'Please don't join us if you're going to be like this. I wish I'd listened to you and cancelled him, to be honest.'

'So do I,' I say. 'Cancel him now. Send him away.'

I know it isn't going to happen.

𝄞

Imran smiles at me as I walk into the kitchen. I wave at him and mouth 'Hello' but say nothing, not wanting to interrupt Stuart, who is sitting with his back to me and is in full flow: 'If I could afford to pay you to do all my neighbours' houses too, believe me, I would. So far I've managed to focus my dissatisfaction on our house looking knackered – and let's face it, at the moment it's the grottiest by some distance – but as soon as you've worked your magic and it looks brilliant, I'm going to start minding the way all the other houses look.'

'Losing battle,' says Imran, his eyes still on me. He is trying to include me because it would be rude not to. I hang back, not yet ready to be part of the conversation. Several sections of this morning's *Sunday Times* lie before Imran in a neat rows-and-columns pattern that makes me think of a card trick. I can guess what's happened: Stuart left them scattered messily on the table as he always does, and Imran felt the need to impose some kind of order.

'Not a battle,' says Stuart. 'A positive-spirited campaign, that's how I like to think of it. Leading by example. Hopefully people'll see how stunning our house looks and think, "Hey, why don't we do that too? It's obviously possible." I think that's it, you know: people assume that if they buy a soot-blackened Victorian house, there's nothing they can do about it — that's just the way it is. It's crazy. They think nothing of ripping out the innards, but getting the outside cleaned? Doesn't seem to occur to anyone, even those who wouldn't dream of letting dirt pile up anywhere else in their house — they're happy to leave more than a hundred years of the city's belched-out waste smeared all over their brickwork. Which ought to be, and once was, yellow! Our voluble next-door neighbour's a perfect example.'

'Of someone who ought to be yellow?' Imran chuckles at his own joke.

'No, of a tosser,' I chip in.

Stuart turns. 'Oh, hi, love. Come and join us.'

I have always admired my husband's optimism, his willingness to leave the bad stuff behind. If only Imran were able to sandblast the crust of dark thoughts and memories off the surface of my brain.

'Do you want a cup of tea?' Stuart asks me.

I nod.

A new day. A new start. Light pours in through the kitchen's two large windows.

If I sit down at the table with Imran, will he notice what's happened to my face? The swollen patches under my eyes have burst and torn the skin. I now have two semicircular red slits, like tiny lipstick grins, one beneath each eye. If I touch them, they start to bleed. And the swellings have not subsided. I've tried to cover the marks with concealer but it hasn't worked as well as I hoped it would.

'I assume Stuart's filled you in?' I say to Imran. 'Our noisy neighbour woes?'

'He has. I feel for you. It's got to be up there in the top five nightmare scenarios.'

Imran likes ranking things. He has ever since university, where the three of us met. One of the first things Stuart and I learned about him was that courgettes are his number one vegetable. I asked him why and he said, 'Isn't it obvious?' Stuart and I still laugh about it.

'You've got to be up there in the top three wild exaggerators,' Stuart says, filling the kettle. 'Noisy neighbours might be nightmare number thirty-five if it's lucky.'

'I knew you'd say that,' Imran crows. 'You're wrong. Top five for sure. Maybe number five, but a solid five — nothing's going to knock it off its spot. And before you start listing murder, torture, rape, fatal illness —'

'Dinner with vegetarians,' I mutter, sitting down opposite Imran at the kitchen table. 'At their house or yours.'

'Right.' Imran nods enthusiastically, as I knew he would. 'Of course all those things are qualitatively worse, but they're not as widespread. You have to take that into account. Not everyone I know's been murdered. Not everyone I know's had a fatal illness —'

'You mean "got" a fatal illness,' says Stuart. 'Because—'

'If I were a political party and I wanted to get elected or re-elected, you know what I'd make my number one policy?' Imran talks over him. 'Any more than three complaints made against anyone for noise that affects neighbours, bang, they're out on the street. No appeal, no due process, nothing. If you rent privately, if you're on housing benefit — out you go. If you own your own home — sorry, it's not yours any more, it's been repossessed.'

'Superb idea.' Stuart winks at me as he hands me my cup of tea.

'You think?' Imran sounds surprised.

'No. But I'm not going to waste my time attacking an opinion you're pretending to hold just to provoke me.'

'I suppose it's too open to abuse.' Imran frowns, criticising himself instead. 'Anyone could pretend their neighbour was noisy just to get rid of them. It would lead to innocent people being culled.'

'You *think*?' Stuart echoes, teasing him. 'Actually, if someone wants to get rid of a next-door neighbour that badly, chances are the neighbour's an arse, like ours is. I was chatting to him the other week about the sandblasting – warning him there'd be some noise and mess. Know what he said, the pompous sod? "It's your decision, obviously, but I'd never have that done. I bought a Victorian house because I love the history, you know? If I'd wanted something shiny and clean, I'd have bought a new-build." As if centuries of grime all over your facade's some kind of period feature, like a ceiling rose or cornicing! I said to Lou, "I bet he'd do it like a shot if he could afford it, but he's spent every last penny on his flash interior." '

Imran opens his mouth to respond, unaware that he's interrupting. We haven't quite reached the end of the story. I know this because I've heard it several times already. The hammering home of the moral is still to come, and it's Stuart's favourite bit. Now, seeing Imran poised to break into his flow, he's going to have to rush it. 'The fact is, this will still be a Victorian house once you've buffed it up,' he says. 'It'll look the way it looked the day it was built – an *unspoiled* Victorian house, restored to its original glory.'

Record time, and word perfect.

A disloyal thought passes through my mind: is this why Stuart has been determined, since we bought 17 Weldon Road, to tackle the outside first and leave the redecorating of inside until later? So that all the neighbours who can't afford to have their brickwork sandblasted, including Mr Fahrenheit, can start to envy us without delay? I wanted to have the inside done first because it's where we live, but Stuart wouldn't hear of it. In the end I capitulated, worried that I might develop an aversion to him if I heard him say 'the fabric of the building' one more time.

'What if Mr Fahrenheit complains about Imran's noise?' I ask him, surprised I didn't think of it before. 'It puts us in a weaker position if our house is generating as much noise during the day as his does at night.'

Imran's shaking his head. 'Everyone has the right to do work to their home during working hours. If he tries to stop you, he'll fail. I've seen it happen time and again. Sometimes council jobsworths come and have a poke around, but I've never been stopped midway through a job and I'm confident I never will be.'

'Lou's got a point, though,' Stuart says. 'This guy works from home a lot. There's no doubt we'll disturb him.' He turns to me. 'Perhaps you should ring the council first thing tomorrow morning and withdraw your complaint.'

'What? Why would I do that?' *Another small grey pebble, poised at the top of the chute, ready for the long roll-down*

'Well, it's hardly fair, is it?' Stuart says. 'Whatever position the council might take, and even if Imran's right, if we're going to subject Fahrenheit to weeks of sandblasting noise, perhaps we should wait to complain until it's over and we're no longer noise pests ourselves. Otherwise it looks hypocritical.'

'No,' says Imran firmly. 'You're comparing two things that aren't equivalent. One's legitimate noise, the other isn't. When it comes to noisy neighbours, you show no mercy. Appeasing them never works.'

'I'm not planning to appease anybody,' I say. *Not Mr Fahrenheit, not my husband and not Imran.* 'I was thinking that maybe we should delay the sandblasting. Or even cancel it altogether.' Since I have made the effort to attend this meeting, I might as well say what I really think. 'I'm sorry, Imran, I know this is the last thing you want to hear, having come all this way –'

'Don't worry about me, Lou. It's no problem at all. I've got jobs to last me two years. Believe me, a cancellation's always welcome –'

'Whoa, hold on!' says Stuart. 'No one's cancelling anything.'

'I might be,' I remind him.

'Lou, you're overreacting. Until all this happened with Fahrenheit—'

'That's irrelevant, Stuart. That was before. It *has* happened, and it's convinced me I don't want to live next door to him. Imran, this is nothing to do with you or your work. I know you'd do a fantastic job, but what's the point in our spending the money, really, if we're not staying?'

'Imran. We're not cancelling you.' Stuart's words

gang up with the tone of his voice to pull rank. As if nothing I've said matters. 'We want you to start as soon as possible, for the very reason Lou gave. It seems we might end up selling the house, if Lou's serious about escaping from Fahrenheit no matter what –'

'Why you do keep saying "Lou" as if it's just me? What about you? Do you want to live next door to a man who persecutes us in the middle of the night with the sound of choirboys?'

'*What?*' says Imran.

Stuart closes his eyes. 'Long story.'

'Well, not *that* long,' I say.

'I'm sure it was just a one-off,' Stuart insists. He obviously doesn't want Imran to hear the story, whatever its length.

'You have no way of knowing that!'

'Even if we decide we want to move, spending thirty grand on the sandblasting now is absolutely the right thing to do. It'll add at least *fifty* grand to the value. Probably more, on a street like this, so close to the station.'

'He's right, Lou. And bear in mind I'm doing this for mate's rates.'

'Right. So, we go ahead. Proceed as planned.'

Stuart drums the flats of his hands on the table, rocking it and spilling my tea. I reach for the section of the *Sunday Times* that's nearest to me, and lay it down over the small beige puddle. I hope it's the news section. I further hope that Stuart hasn't read it yet and now won't be able to.

The liquid soaks all the way through to the top, despite the segment of newspaper being several pages thick. I turn it over and see that it's the property section – my favourite. I haven't read it yet and now won't be able to. Does what goes around normally come around so quickly?

'So you're prepared to be in the dark for a while?' Imran asks.

'In the dark?' I say.

He looks at Stuart, puzzled. 'You didn't tell her?'

'It went right out of my head, I'm afraid. It won't be for long, will it? And I mean . . . we've got electricity. And candles in the event of a power cut.'

'So?' I stare at him. 'Now that you've remembered, are you going to tell me what you're talking about?'

Stuart looks at Imran, who says, 'There's going to be scaffolding up all round the house. You knew that, right?'

I nod.

'We're going to need to cover the scaffolding with thick plastic sheeting, front and back, and cover the windows with cardboard, tape them up. You're not going to be seeing much natural daylight until we're finished, I'm afraid. But hopefully since you're at work all day it won't make that much difference. And with the nights drawing in —'

'No natural daylight,' I repeat, looking at Stuart. I'm very aware of my heartbeat, suddenly. *He wants to bury us alive.* I feel as if it's happened already. The room seems darker than it did a few seconds ago.

'That's the advantage of the nights drawing in,' Imran says cheerfully. What is? I missed it, if there was one. I didn't hear anything I liked the sound of. 'Disadvantage is, the job's going to take a lot longer than it would in summer, because we can't work in the dark. So I'm afraid you're going to be stuck with our scaffolding and sheeting for a while.'

'Can't you do it in sections?' I ask. 'Cover the windows one floor at a time, or do the back first and then the front?'

'Sorry,' Imran says. 'It's just not the way we work.'

'Even if customers want you to work a different way?'

'Lou,' Stuart mutters.

'It'd double the costs if we had to get the scaffolders out twice,' says Imran.

'Then we'll pay double!'

'No, we won't,' says Stuart. 'Lou, don't be crazy. It'll be fine. Like Imran says, you're at work all day —'

'Not at weekends! And what about the Christmas holidays? Joseph will be home then.' I turn to Imran. 'Will you be finished by the fourteenth of December? I'm not bringing my son home to a house with no natural light. I'm not! I'll tear the plastic sheeting off myself if I have to.'

'It's unlikely to be finished that soon,' says Imran. 'Sandblasting's a fiddly job if you do it right — and I'm a perfectionist. Look, call me oversensitive, but the vibe I'm getting isn't one of unbridled enthusiasm. Maybe you two need to—'

'We need to go ahead and get it done,' Stuart insists, cutting him off.

It isn't only the light that we'll lose. The views will go too. Nothing but blackness at every window.

'There must be an alternative,' I say, panic building inside me. 'I'm not agreeing to this if it means living wrapped up in a dark box for months. I'll move out! You can live in the dark on your own,' I snap at Stuart.

'Lou.' He puts his hand over mine. Looks worried. 'You're tired, and you're massively overreacting.'

'You are a bit, Lou,' Imran agrees. 'I've been doing this for years. People get used to the no-light thing. Honestly – you'll be surprised how soon it seems normal. And if we don't do it, we'll have people queuing up to complain within half an hour of us starting the work. If you were in the depths of the countryside with no neighbours for miles around, we could forget the sheeting and you could keep your light, but . . .' He shrugs.

Countryside: the word lodges in my brain. I heard it very recently. Where? No, I didn't hear it; I read it. On wet newsprint.

I look down at the tea-stained *Sunday Times* 'Home' supplement in front of me and see a full-page advertisement for something called Swallowfield: 'Where Putting Nature First is Second Nature'. No, that can't be right. Swallowfield must be its name, whatever it is, and the rest is advertising. 'The perfect peaceful countryside retreat, only two hours from London.' There's a background picture of fields at dusk, separated by hedges; a row of trees in the distance; a sunset of purple and orange streaks. On top of this, blocking out parts of the idyllic scene, are three other pictures in small boxes: a woman's bare tanned back with a row of round black stones dotting her spine and a white towel covering her obviously toned bottom; a large outdoor swimming pool with water that looks dark green and stone fountains at its four corners pouring new water into it; and a long, one-storey house that seems to be made almost wholly of glass with only the odd strip of metal holding all the glass together. The caption reads: 'Our award-winning Glass House'. It's beautiful. Like a jewel, with nothing around it but green emptiness.

I like all the words I can see on this page. I like them a lot more than what Stuart and Imran are saying.

A gated second-home community in the Culver Valley. That might be two hours from London – a little bit more, actually, more like two and a half – but it's only an hour from Cambridge.

The perfect peaceful countryside retreat.

Our heated outdoor green slate 25-metre swimming pool, open to residents and their guests 365 days a year.

A hot stone treatment at our award-winning £10-million Lumina Spa.

There's a phone number. For a sales office. I tear

my eyes away and look up, aware that I don't want to get caught. Now my heart is beating too fast not with dread but because of a phone number. I wonder why I feel guilty. Since the number doesn't belong to another man, I have no reason to.

Imran is still talking. 'It's up to you if you want to take the risk,' he says, 'but on a street like this, with people waiting to jump down our throats if we put a foot wrong, I'd suggest we wrap you up good and tight, or else there'll be dust clouds in all your neighbours' houses and spilling out all over the road. Did Stuart warn you about the dust?'

'No. He didn't.'

'I'm sure I *did*.'

'How much dust?' I ask.

'A not insignificant amount,' Imran says earnestly. 'We'll do our best to protect you by taping up the windows as thoroughly as we can, but ... realistically, you're going to be living with dust for a while.'

Dust. Taped-up windows. No air, no light. This is how I might be warned about death – in exactly this way, with qualifications like 'realistically' and 'not insignificant'. As if nothing horrifying is about to take place. Terror lands in my heart from nowhere, without warning, and grips me. For a few seconds I can't breathe or speak. Silently, in my head, I recite what I hope are the magic words, and what Stuart would say: *One day the work on my house will end and, when it does, the light will return and the dust will go away.*

I have to make it clear to Stuart that the sandblasting can't happen. Later, when Imran's gone. He has already witnessed more than enough marital disharmony.

The perfect peaceful countryside retreat.

'I promise you, Lou – it'll be worth it,' he says. Stuart nods along.

Where putting nature first is second nature.

'I know.' I realise too late that I shouldn't have said that, but my mind is busy trying to memorise Swallowfield's phone number.

Dr Ivan Freeman, Saviour College School's director of music, has the kind of beard I hate. It's tidy and shaped and dense, as if someone has fitted a rust-coloured carpet with a high pile count around his mouth. I see it every Sunday morning, and also on Tuesday and Thursday evenings. During term time it is not possible for me to see my son without seeing Dr Freeman's beard at the same time. I've started to dread its appearance, even though the first sighting of it on any given day means that I will soon see Joseph. I'm trying to picture it now, before Dr Freeman and the choir arrive, to prepare myself.

Stuart and I are sitting where we always sit in Saviour's chapel on Sundays, Tuesdays and Thursdays. All the choirboy parents have fixed places that they rush to as soon as the chapel doors open: the ones that offer the best views of their sons, each of whom always stands in precisely the same spot to sing.

Our sons.

We, the parents, arrive first: before our boys and before the rest of the congregation. We hurry into the cold, silent chapel, not giving a toss about its beautiful stained-glass windows or the elaborate woodcarvings on its centuries-old panelled walls because those things have nothing to do with our children, and we sit on hard benches, awaiting the agonising proximity. We're excited because we're about to be close to our sons for a short while, and already devastated because we know this blissful state will last only forty-five minutes, or an hour, or two hours if there's a buffet lunch afterwards as there is today.

And we won't be close enough; we'll be trapped, by custom and politeness, in our pews, several metres away, unable to hug our boys as we yearn to: audience, not participants. Dr Freeman will be closer. When today's festivities are over, he will lead our sons away into the recesses of the school, and we won't see them again until the next service.

Perhaps not all the parents feel the way I do. I know Stuart doesn't. He's always delighted to see Joseph, but ready and willing to say goodbye to him when the time comes. *As long as he's happy, Lou, I'm happy, and he's quite clearly in his element.*

I don't want Joseph to be in his element. I want him to be in his house. Sleeping in his bed every night.

It would sound sexist, so I never say it, but I don't care how Stuart or any of the fathers feel. They're men. It's different. I wonder about the mothers: how many of them loathe the set-up as much as I do? I'm particularly suspicious of the ones who stridently parrot the lines we've all been fed by Dr Freeman, the chaplain and the headmaster about how lucky we all are and how grateful we ought to be. I secretly hope that one day one of them will crack — ideally during an important service — and scream abuse at the top of her lungs before grabbing her son and making a run for it.

I only know three of the mothers by name: Celia Morris, Donna McSorley and Alexis Grant. All of them arrived before me today for the first time. This bothers me. I want to be first into the chapel, always, seconds after the doors open to the public. I want the chaplain to notice that I come earlier and wait longer than anyone else, and I want him to pass this information on to Dr Freeman, who, if he's ever tempted to release one boy only, like a terrorist holding a room full of hostages at gunpoint in an action movie, might be more likely to choose Joseph if he's heard about my extended, devoted vigils.

I know this is superstitious rubbish; I might as well believe in elves or fairies. Dr Freeman isn't as willing to compromise as the average Hollywood hostage-taker, who has his crazed and trigger-happy moments, true, but who ultimately is usually prepared to set free the occasional frail old man or pregnant woman.

I noticed Alexis Grant smirking as Stuart and I hurried in, cutting it fine thanks to our meeting with Imran. She's worked out that I like to be earlier than early, and is pleased that on this occasion I've messed up.

I knew I didn't like Alexis ten minutes into my first conversation with her. She asked me where I lived and, when I said Weldon Road, she pulled a face and said, 'Oh, poor you, stuck in the centre of Cambridge. Have you got one of those big Victorian town houses?' Without giving me a chance to reply, she went on: 'Let me guess – a maintenance nightmare? With a tiny garden, right?' I told her we didn't have a garden as such – only a small courtyard – and watched the delight spread across her face. 'We've got two acres,' she said proudly. 'In Orwell. I wouldn't swap it for anything.' I thought, but didn't say, that I wasn't offering to swap. When I told Stuart later, he snorted and said, 'There's *one* thing you can say in Orwell's favour. Only one. It's close to Cambridge. That's it.'

Celia Morris is less obnoxious than Alexis, but equally irritating. She's a timid, insecure woman who seems prepared to worship, instantly, anyone who dares to express an opinion, or, indeed, to do anything. Shortly after meeting me, she got it into her head that I was a brave warrior who feared nothing and no one – I've no idea on what basis she formed this opinion – and now whenever she sees me she says the same thing in a new way: 'Look at me, I'm soaked! I forgot my umbrella. I'm so useless. You probably never forget your umbrella, do you? I bet the rain wouldn't dare to fall on you even if you did.' Or: 'I would kiss you hello but I've got a streaming cold. I'm not like you – you probably never get ill. Look at you, you're the picture of health.' She makes these absurd pronouncements in a tone of deep admiration, with a fawning smile on her face, and if I try to point out that I'm capable of getting as wet or sick as the next person, she smiles even more adoringly and says, 'I can't believe how modest you are.' I would love to say to her one day, 'Celia, you know literally nothing about me. What on earth are you talking about?' She would either burst into tears and run from the room, or giggle affectionately and say, 'You're so funny. I wish I had a sense of humour like yours.'

Donna McSorley is by far the best of the three: a plump solicitor with an apparently endless supply of too-tight suits that show a lot of cleavage, and chaotic hair that she always wears not entirely down and not entirely up, with lots of bands and clips and bits sprouting out at odd angles, like a character from a Dr Seuss book. She has an enormous mountain of a second husband who dresses like an aristocrat-turned-vagrant — expensive but scruffy — and whom she clearly adores. The first time he came to a choir service, she propelled him towards me, one hand on his back and one on his stomach, calling out, 'Louise! Have you met my lovely man?' They giggled and kissed while the boys were singing.

I would never admit it to a single soul, but it bothers me that Donna, whom I hardly know, has a new husband that she is so enthusiastic about. I'm jealous of her second helpings. I don't want to divorce Stuart, but, all other things being equal, I think — no, I know — that I would love to have a second husband I adored enough to introduce to people as 'my lovely man', with my hand on his belly. I would like to have the chance to choose a husband now that I'm older and know how expertly I would choose, leaving nothing to chance.

According to Alexis Grant, Donna's first husband was a disaster: violent, alcoholic, unfaithful, racist.

All the bad things. 'Did she add "unimpressed by Orwell"?' Stuart asked when I relayed this information. I smile as I remember laughing at the time. My first husband is witty and clever and loves me. He doesn't drink too much, doesn't cheat on me, isn't violent, isn't racist, seems always to be in the same stable good mood. He has a steady and important job that I'm in awe of: Applications Group Manager for the Cambridge Crystallographic Data Centre. Alexis didn't like it when I told her that. Her own fault: if she hadn't demanded to know why we'd chosen to live in the noisy centre of the city, I wouldn't have been forced to mention Stuart's two-minute walk to work and what that work was.

The organ starts to play. My heart springs up in my chest. This means Joseph is here: outside, in the antechapel. We wait. The minutes feel like weeks. Then the doors to the main chapel open and Dr Freeman walks in, with his carpet-beard, smiling an I've-got-all-your-sons smile. Two columns of sombre-faced boys follow him in, dressed in red cassocks with white surplices over the top and holding black files full of today's hymns, songs and prayers. I am desperate to catch a glimpse of Joseph, but I know it will be a while before he moves into view. As a junior probationer, he is at the back of the line. When he finally appears, I gasp. He looks healthy and happy. Radiant. Stuart puts a restraining hand on my arm. *It's okay*, I want to say to him. *I'm not going to do anything crazy.*

Joseph smiles up at us. I smile back and wave. At this point Stuart always looks at me anxiously, to check I'm not crying, and today is no exception. A few of the mothers always cry, smiling furiously at the same time to make it clear that these are happy aren't-we-lucky tears, not the kind that are likely to cause problems for the school.

My eyes are swollen, with red-mouthed wound-grins beneath them, but dry. Crying would be too risky. There's a fiery ball of outrage inside me that would blind me if I were to let any of it pour out. Dr Freeman would only need to catch one glimpse and he would guess that I'm secretly plotting the destruction of his career, Saviour College, its school, its choir, its reputation – everything it has worked for hundreds of years to consolidate.

Joseph's hair shines. His shoes are scuffed. His face, pale and oval-shaped, draws all the light in the chapel to it and is the only one I see. Beside him, all the other boys look like cardboard cut-outs.

When the chaplain starts to sing the Opening Responses, I tear my eyes away from my son and look up and down the pews to check that Mr Fahrenheit isn't here. Silly; why would he be?

Because it's another thing he could do to intimidate you: a variation on a theme.

Some elements of the service are always the same, and these are by far my favourite bits. I am starting to think of them as part of my son. I have no choice but to love them if he's singing them whenever I see him. Not the psalm: that's different every time. Today, it contains a line explicitly stating that only he who does no evil to his neighbour will sojourn in the Lord's holy tent. *Hear that, Mr Fahrenheit? No holy tent for you, just a great big theological 'Fuck Off' sign at the entrance flap.*

After the reading of the psalm, the chaplain says, 'Let us now offer to God our prayers and petitions.' Like the Opening Responses, this is a regular feature, but I don't love it because Joseph isn't part of it — it's one of the chaplain's solo pieces. No tune either.

'This morning we pray for the sick and the injured. We pray for Betty Carter, Andrew Saunders, Heather Aspinall ...'

I block out the names, and pray only for my son to be allowed to come home with me today after the service.

'We pray for the recently deceased, and in particular, for the repose of the souls of Dennis Halliday, Timothy Laws, Edith Kelly . . .'

I pray that Joseph will suddenly be found to be tone-deaf, so that he can no longer be a member of Saviour College boys' choir. So that he can be sent home.

'. . . We pray for peace on earth, but also for the establishment of justice, without which there can be no peace.'

'That's debatable,' I whisper to Stuart.

'Ssh,' he says.

'Peace will have to stand on its own two feet, since no one's ever going to agree on a definition of justice, let alone bring it into being.'

'Can we discuss this later?'

'I hate the way he veers from the sad death of a congregation member's auntie or gran to global misery and . . . massive abstract platitudes,' I mutter. I say this every Sunday. On Tuesdays and Thursdays, for variety, I bitch about the words of the endlessly repeated Magnificat: 'He hath filled the hungry with good things, and the rich he hath sent empty away.' It sounds vindictive, and makes no sense, because those sent empty away will soon constitute the new hungry. Will the Lord feed them then? How hungry would they have to be to qualify? Does God want everyone to be equally well fed, or is he more interested in punishing the privileged for their good fortune thus far? That's certainly how it sounds, especially in conjunction with 'He hath put down the mighty from their seat'. Are we to assume God has Bolshevik tendencies?

I'm prepared to concede that whoever wrote those lines of the Magnificat probably didn't intend them to sound as bad as they do, but still – a quick edit could have solved the problem. 'He hath filled the hungry with good things, and the rich he hath pointed in the direction of a Michelin-starred restaurant, knowing they'll be well catered for there.'

'Lord in thy mercy . . .' intones the chaplain.

That's our cue. 'Hear our prayer,' we all say in unison. I like that bit: saying the same words as my son. I try to breathe in his breath from across the room.

'We pray for individuals who have asked for our prayers, and for those for whom prayers have been asked by others: Cath and Dan Taylor, Margaret, Elsie . . .'

Worried he's upset me by trying to shut me up, Stuart leans over and whispers, 'I bet Elsie's the one who's asked for the prayer for herself. She sounds like a rampant egotist.'

I smile.

'On the anniversaries of their deaths, we pray for Nora Wallis, Anne Dobson, Peter Turner, Emma Kobayashi. Lord in thy mercy . . .'

'Hear our prayer.'

Stuart says into my ear, '"We pray for the prosecution of Mr Fahrenheit, who has totally asked for it with his crap and inconsiderate behaviour over several months." I dare you to write that in the big blue prayer book on your way out.'

'I'd do it,' I whisper back. 'Would you?'

'I might.'

'I dare you.'

'All right. I will. If you promise never to tell Joseph. Have you mentioned Mr Fahrenheit to anyone connected with Saviour? By that name?'

'I've not mentioned him at all.'

'Good. Then there's no way they can link it with Joseph.'

SOPHIE HANNAH

'You're not really going to do it, are you?'

'Why not?' says Stuart. 'I'll disguise my writing.'

'There's no way he'd ever read it out, even if you left out the word "crap".'

'Doesn't matter,' Stuart whispers. 'Once it's in the big blue book, it's between me and the Lord.'

I stifle a giggle. Joseph gives me a pointed look: his embarrassing mother.

I love my husband a little bit more than I did when we arrived. For the first time in this chapel since Joseph started at Saviour, and thanks to Stuart, I was separated from my anger and misery for long enough to laugh.

'Imagine if I murdered Fahrenheit and wrote his name in the blue book under "Recent Deaths RIP",' Stuart says quietly behind his hand. '*That'd get read out.* You'd hear the chaplain praying for the repose of the soul of Justin Clay and you'd turn to me in astonishment. Then you'd see the look in my eyes — the knowing glint — and you'd realise I'd killed him, and this was my way of telling you — I'd have used the chaplain as a conduit for my confession, without his knowledge.'

'And then I'd stand up and shout, "May his soul burn in hell",' I suggest, not liking my passive role in Stuart's story. Which isn't to say that I don't like it as a whole; I do. I don't care if he's going all out to please me, and only because he feels guilty about the sandblasting and the dust and his ability to sleep through noise. He has a talent for making me want to forgive him.

This is why God, if he exists, will never allocate me a second husband. Donna only got one because her first was so unremittingly awful. That must be the deal: you either get an execrable one followed by a second who is close to perfection, or you get one for life who makes you feel abandoned and let down one minute, and rescued from painful exile the next.

I'm not sure I still wouldn't rather swap my deal for Donna's.

♪

The buffet is in Saviour's cavernous and subterranean Old Kitchen. It's high-quality boring: the best vol-au-vents and little sausages, the creamiest coleslaw, the most expensive chicken legs, quiches and sliced baguettes, but nothing I couldn't have predicted, and not only because it's identical to every other Saviour buffet I've attended.

We parents are waiting for our sons again. Joseph and the other choristers and probationers are getting changed out of their cassocks and surplices, into what they call their 'play clothes'. It's another part of the routine that I resent. What does it matter what they're wearing? Give them to us, O Lord, for ten minutes longer.

'I'm not sure I can eat this lunch again,' I complain to Alexis, whose one useful characteristic is that if you feel like bitching about something, she usually joins in enthusiastically.

'It's Groundhog Lunch,' she says. Dr Freeman is chortling loudly on the other side of the room, through his Groundhog Beard. A circle of parents has gathered round him. It includes my treacherous husband.

'Next time, I'm going to bring my own supplies from the Botanic Gardens café,' I tell Alexis as I pick up a vol-au-vent I have no appetite for and put it on my plate.

'You don't like it there, do you?' She wrinkles her nose.

'I love it. I go most days for lunch. The food's really different, in a good way. Last time I went, I had sweet potato and cottage cheese salad – it was delicious.'

'If you say so. Sounds gross to me. You're making me like the look of those chicken legs a whole lot more.' She laughs, picks one up with a paper napkin and starts to nibble at it.

I ought to drop the subject, but I can't resist saying, 'The Botanics café also does soup, pork pie, lovely cakes – do you like any of those? And you can sit and eat with a fantastic view of beautiful gardens. You like gardens, don't you?'

'I can look at my own garden for free, thank you very much. Four quid a time, just to get through the gates, when it used to be free? No, thanks.'

Alexis is as predictable as Saviour's buffets. She can't admit that the Botanic Gardens have anything worthwhile to offer because they're in Cambridge. Also counting against them is their proximity to my house and to my office, which reminds Alexis, presumably, that she's stuck out in Orwell, miles from where she and her husband work, at KPMG. Coincidentally, that's also very close to the Botanic Gardens: just across Hills Road.

'She'd be a lot happier if she just admitted she'd love to live in Cambridge but can't afford to,' Stuart has said more than once. 'You should tell her.'

'Here are the boys!' a female voice calls out, and

then they flood in, running towards their parents. All over the room, small arms fling themselves round waists. Not Joseph's; he's heading for the buffet, shouting, 'Hi, Mum! Hi, Dad!' with his eyes on the cocktail sausages. I walk over to him and give him a big hug, hardly able to bear the joy and pain that spring up inside me: the way each recoils like the head of a snake as it senses the presence of the other and prepares to fight to the death, having forgotten that this always ends the same way; the winner is always the same – less deserving but stronger.

Does it ever get any easier? I could ask some of the older choristers' mothers, but I'm afraid to, in case they look puzzled and say, 'Why, are you finding it difficult?' and make me feel like a freak.

Perhaps Stuart's right. Perhaps I'm too invested in Joseph, too dependent on him. Except, in my defence, I'm sure I wouldn't be if only I had the standard eighteen years in which to learn to let go. No one warned me I'd have to do it in seven.

'You were brilliant, darling,' I say, holding on to him. He wriggles free. I never used to do this: crush him against my body at every opportunity and keep him there too long, so that he feels he has to escape.

Saviour College School has created the problem of my clinginess; this time last year, it didn't exist.

'You always say I'm brilliant, Mum. Because you're my mum.' He seems fine. Happy. Exactly as he used to be. No harm has come to him. That's good; I can use it to console myself later, when he's gone.

'You're always brilliant, that's why,' I say. All around me, I hear parents saying the same thing to their sons. I wonder how many of them have wished for sudden tone-deafness to put an end to the brilliance. None as acutely as I have, I'm sure.

'Mum, you know you said I wasn't allowed to have high-tops?'

'What?'

Joseph grabs a handful of small sausages and tries to put them all in his mouth at once. One falls to the floor. I cover it with my foot and crush it into the carpet.

'Mum!' Joseph chastises me, looking left and right to check no one noticed. 'And you and Dad were talking during the service! I saw you.'

'Sorry,' I say.

'I'll let you off if you buy me some high-tops,' he says hopefully.

'What are they?'

'You know, those trainers I wanted from Sports Direct – you said you'd read somewhere that they're bad for your feet or your ankles? Well, they're not. Louis wears high-tops all the time and he says it's not true. I've seen his feet and ankles and there's nothing wrong with them.' Louis is Donna McSorley's son. Like Joseph, he's a junior probationer.

It would be too easy to say, 'There's nothing wrong with his feet and ankles *yet*, but you watch – he's sure to be disfigured in later life because he wore the wrong trainers.' I don't know if there's anything dangerous about high-tops and I never did; I added a half-remembered rumour about the lace-up knee-length boots I wore as a teenage Goth to my desire to leave Sports Direct as soon as possible; the ankle-and-foot-damage line was what I came up with. I can't admit this, so I say, 'You can probably have some high-tops, yes. Maybe for Christmas.'

'Really?' Joseph looks astonished. 'Epic!'

'What's epic?' Stuart asks, joining us. He ruffles Joseph's hair: a typical 'affectionate father' gesture that could have come from a manual. I want a demonstration of my husband's passionate love for our son, not something that looks as if it's been inspired by a building society advertisement.

Alexis Grant tugs at my sleeve. 'You're number nineteen Weldon Road, aren't you?' she says.

'No. Seventeen. Why?'

She taps the screen of her iPhone. 'Christmas card list,' she says.

I don't believe her. If she wanted to send me a Christmas card she could hand it to me after a choir service any time between now and 25 December.

'Well, if you're delivering by hand, there's no number on the door. Just look for the dirtiest, most pollution-stained house on the street.'

She perks up like a dog at the mention of walkies, eager to hear me list more of my house's faults.

'Still, not for long.' I proceed swiftly to my punchline: 'We've having the brickwork cleaned, starting a week tomorrow. It'll look amazing once that's done.'

'My mum says I can have some high-tops for Christmas,' Joseph tells Nathan and another boy who has wandered over: Sebby, I think. I don't know his surname.

'Epic,' they both say in unison. Then Sebby turns to Nathan and says, 'Jinx padlock!'

'You've been padlocked,' Joseph tells Nathan, as if this is something serious and final that cannot be revoked.

My son has become bilingual in the languages of school and home.

I see Dr Freeman approaching and feel my skeleton stiffen, as if its hardness can protect me from the inside. Instead of saying, 'Hello, Mrs Beeston,' or 'Hi, Louise,' he says, 'And here's Joseph's mum,' as he sidles up to me. I would so love to reply, 'And here's Joseph's choirmaster.'

'The boys did well this morning,' I say instead.

'Didn't they?' Dr Freeman beams. 'I think it was the best service so far this term. They've made amazing progress in only a few weeks – it's incredible, actually.'

I wouldn't go that far. They sang a few songs. Nicely. How hard can it be?

'Our junior probationers are quick learners this year. It makes a big difference. Joseph's coming on in leaps and bounds.'

'That's great to hear,' Stuart gushes. 'Working hard, is he?'

'I could probably work harder,' Joseph says.

'He's extremely committed,' says Dr Freeman,

and my son looks relieved. 'All the new boys are. It's wonderful. Don't let all this praise go to your head, young man.' He pats Joseph on the shoulder, then turns to me. 'I know it's hard for parents at first, but I hope you can see there's no need to worry, Mrs Beeston. Joseph's blossoming.'

'Yes, he seems...' This is the most I can manage, and it nearly chokes me. It will have to do. In order to avoid looking at Dr Freeman, I turn to my left and stare at Alexis's back instead. She's talking to the organ scholar, Tobias, about something he has applied for or is about to apply for.

Blossoming. He could have said 'getting along fine' or 'settling in nicely', but he chose to say 'blossoming' instead: a word that brings to mind a flower suddenly bathed in light and water, with plenty of room to grow after years of confinement in suboptimal conditions. The arrogance takes my breath away.

'Oh, I can Google it for you,' Alexis says to Tobias. Before she has a chance to key anything in, I see the screen of her phone over her shoulder. On it is my address, the price Stuart and I paid for our house and the purchase date. I read the line beneath and see that number 27 Weldon Road sold in November 2011 for £989,950. To the Shamirs. It doesn't say that on Alexis's phone, but I know Salma Shamir; we go to the same yoga class.

It takes me a few seconds, but I get there in the end: a sold-house prices website. I've heard about them, but never seen one before.

I tap Alexis on the shoulder blade and she turns round. 'We'd have gone up to one point five million if we'd had to,' I say in a matey, confiding voice, nodding at her phone's screen. Since she seems at a loss for words, I help her out by saying, 'In your shoes, I'd still send me a Christmas card, however embarrassing it might be. Not sending one'd be worse.'

I turn back to Dr Freeman and Stuart, who are talking about a national classical composition prize for under-twelves. Joseph, Nathan and Sebby have wandered off to the far end of the buffet table where the cakes are. I wait for a gap in the conversation and say, 'I've been thinking about the boarding thing.'

Stuart widens his eyes at me: a clear 'Stop' signal.

'The boarding requirement. For choristers,' I clarify.

'Yes.' Dr Freeman looks solemn. 'I know you had

your reservations when we spoke in the summer –'

'Only that it's taken to such an extreme. I don't mind the idea of boarding per se, but I was wondering – would it be possible to consider a minor modification to the system, to reflect more of a balance?' I smile brightly. Stuart will tell me later that I wasted my breath and made a fool of myself; I ought to know that no aspect of the Saviour College choirboy routine has changed since the early 1700s. I should infer from this, as everyone else seems to, that it never will.

'Balance?' says Dr Freeman. The expression on his face – one of genuine open-minded enquiry – is flawless. From years of practice, no doubt. I can't believe I'm the first mother to suggest change, or complain.

'Yes, between the school's need to have the boys on site as much as possible and the need for them to have a proper home life,' I say. 'I mean, what if during term time they boarded for four nights a week and lived at home for three, for example? They could still have choir practice four out of seven mornings before school – mightn't that be enough?'

'Ah. Oh, dear.' Dr Freeman smiles sympathetically.

'I'm sorry if you're finding it hard to adjust to Joseph not being at home. It really will get easier, you know.'

'Yes, but one way to make it easier would be to change the rules, wouldn't it?' I say. 'Just because something's always been done one way—'

'We believe it's for a sound reason, Mrs Beeston. The choirboys have so much on their plates – so much more than our non-chorister pupils, probably double the workload. It just wouldn't be feasible for them to be ferried back and forth from home to school every day, I'm afraid –'

'I didn't say every day –'

'It would be so disruptive.'

'What about five, two then? Five nights at school, two at home.'

'They need the boys living at school during term time, Lou,' Stuart intervenes. 'Otherwise they wouldn't make it a requirement.'

'I accept that you and Dr Freeman think that, darling, and that you might be right and I might be wrong,' I say in a Sunday-best voice that I've never used before. Nor have I ever called Stuart 'darling', nor sided against him with people who are trying to steal his child for no good reason. 'What I'm asking is — is it possible to get this on to some kind of . . . school agenda, so that it can be debated by everyone with a stake, including the parents and the boys? If I'm outvoted, I'll concede defeat, but I think it's something that ought to be reviewed.'

'Mrs Beeston, I really wouldn't want to raise your hopes —'

'You haven't. And I'm sure you won't.'

'Give it a few more weeks. I'd be very surprised if you didn't feel happier by then.'

'You're misunderstanding me. You don't need to worry about my emotional state — that's my responsibility, not yours.'

'Lou, for God's sake. I'm sorry, Dr Freeman.'

'For what?' I ask. 'Taking the Lord's name in vain, or me asking a reasonable question?'

'It's quite all right, Mr Beeston. No need to apologise.'

'It's a simple procedural question, Dr Freeman. How would I go about raising this as a topic for discussion, so that opinions can be solicited from all the appropriate parties?'

'There's always Jesus College,' Alexis suggests from behind me. 'The Jesus choristers all live at home.'

I didn't realise she was listening.

Everyone is listening.

'It's not the same,' says a mother whose name I don't know. She sounds nervous. 'They don't get the same fully rounded experience. Nipping to choir a few times a week's not the same.'

Dr Freeman says, 'Jesus has an excellent choir. Of course, I think ours is far superior, but then I'm biased.' He chuckles. 'Now, parents, do come and help yourselves to more food before your sons eat it all.'

Please, sir, can we have some more? As Oliver Twist might have said. He was a boarder.

The five or six faces that looked anxious a few seconds ago have reverted to bland, smiling normality; Dr Freeman made a couple of light-hearted remarks and now all is right in the world of the choir mothers once again.

They would all vote against me. Even Donna, probably. Because of history, because of tradition. If one day Dr Freeman announced that, thanks to advances in science, it was now possible to dig up the original sixteen Saviour choirboys from 1712, the first intake, and re-power their voices using fragments of DNA found in their burial soil, the choir mothers would probably all vote in favour of that too, even if it meant their sons would have to be sacked as choristers. 'I do love the sense of history you get here,' they would warble from their cold pews in chapel as the sound of the Magnificat rose from sixteen piles of grey bone dust.

When Dr Freeman next looks in my direction, I take the uneaten vol-au-vent off my plate and put it down on the buffet table beside a large bowl of fruit salad.

♪

Stuart turns the car in to Weldon Road, then pulls in by the kerb several hundred metres from our house. We have driven this far in complete silence.

'Why are we stopping here? I thought we were going home. Home's up there.' I point.

'Do you want to tell me what the hell you thought you were playing at?' he asks.

'I want to go home. This isn't some kind of Mafia-style hit you and Dr Freeman have arranged, is it?'

'Don't be ridiculous.'

'Sorry. I didn't realise jokes were forbidden.'

'Did I say that?' he snaps.

I decide to put it to the test. 'Everyone knows what happens to women who say too much to the wrong people. They're driven to unexpected destinations by men who won't look them in the eye, and then shot.'

It has started to rain again. It is also sunny, in a cold, bright, white way: jagged shiny patches all over the sky. If Joseph were here, I would tell him to look for a rainbow.

'I asked you a serious question,' says my serious husband.

'If you mean what I said to Dr Freeman, I wasn't playing at anything. I dared to suggest that something might change, that's all. For the better.'

'I don't want to get a reputation as a troublemaker, Lou.'

I laugh. 'I don't think there's much danger of that. I'm sure you're already well established in Dr Freeman's mind as the pushover of his dreams.'

'You *were* only asking, I suppose. Dr Freeman surely can't hold that against us, can he? At least you were straightforward.'

This must have been going on all the way home, inside his head: his argument with himself about how culpable I am. I should keep out of the discussion, since I'm hardly impartial.

I can't.

'He has our son, Stuart. He has him right now. We don't, and won't until the fourteenth of December at four o'clock. I think that gives me the right to ask a few questions, don't you?'

'Probably,' Stuart says grudgingly, as if he wishes it weren't the case. 'I'd hate to think he'd . . . I don't know, take against you and take it out on Joseph in some way.'

'If you think that's a possibility, you should have insisted on bringing Joseph home with us after lunch.'

'Based on what? Some groundless fear?'

Based on the principle that you remove your son from the control of a man you don't trust.

'Look, fair enough – you wanted to ask your question and you asked it –'

'And was ignored.'

'No, you got your answer – nothing's going to change. And, frankly, I think you either accept that, or—'

'Did you write anything in the prayer book, about Mr Fahrenheit?' I ask.

Stuart frowns at the interruption. 'What's that got to do with anything?'

'You said you would.'

'Well... I will at some point, yes. Frankly, I couldn't give a toss about Fahrenheit at the moment. I'm talking about our son's education, our family – that's more important. Lou, if we want to get on with our life in any kind of sane and functional way, your attitude to Saviour's going to have to—'

'Change,' I cut him short. 'I agree. I think there's a way I might be able to feel okay about things.'

'Really?'

It's time for my pitch, the one I've been preparing all the way home. I didn't expect to have to present it so soon; at the same time, I can see the advantage of putting it to Stuart here in the car rather than inside the house. It feels more appropriate somehow.

'You and Dr Freeman are right. Joseph's thriving. Happy. He seems to have settled in very quickly.' It pains me to admit this. 'And... Saviour's demonstrably one of the best schools in the country, and he's got a free place there. It would be wrong to pull him out just because I hate him not living at home. Selfish.'

'Yesss,' Stuart hisses with relief. How lonely

it must have been for him, waiting for me to be reasonable. As lonely as it was for me. If he had made any concession to my feelings, even the tiniest, I would never have attained this level of rationality.

I would never have reached the point of coldly evaluating my bargaining power.

'So Joseph can stay — at the school and in the choir. Which will make you and Dr Freeman happy, right?'

'It should make you happy too,' says Stuart.

'It possibly should, but it doesn't,' I tell him briskly. 'But let's not give up too easily. Maybe something else could make me happy, or at least happier. I need something, Stuart. However wonderful an opportunity Saviour is for Joseph, I feel as if I've suffered a devastating loss.'

'Loss?' If he could trap the word in a net and haul it away, he would. 'Isn't that a bit strong? Joseph's only down the road, not on another continent. We see him three times a week —'

'I know the situation.' I raise my voice to block out his words. 'If I can't have my way, at least allow me to have my feelings.'

'I'm trying to make you feel better!'

It depresses me to think that this might be true.

Is my husband really so ineffectual? I'd prefer to think of him as skilfully selfish. 'It's different for you,' I say. 'You've got what you want – Joseph at Saviour, the sandblasting of the house –'

Stuart laughs. 'What do you mean, I've "got" the sandblasting of the house? That's a means to an end that benefits us both. It's your house too.'

'I've given way on two things that really matter to me – my seven-year-old son effectively leaving home, and the revamp of the outside of the house, which I would very much like to cancel, except you won't let me. So ... you've won. Twice.'

'That's absurd. It's not a competition, for goodness' sake!'

I can't decide if he's being modest or unappreciative.

'You won,' I repeat. 'I'd rather Joseph lived at home and joined Jesus College choir instead. I'd rather have sooty brickwork like everyone else on the street, and not have to live without natural light for months, in a dust-trap. Also – and I know this isn't an instance of you winning in quite the same way but it still counts – you're not disturbed by Mr Fahrenheit's noise when it happens. I am.'

'I'm not sure what you're saying, Lou.'

That's because I haven't said it yet.

'Or why you're being so . . . weird and cold. Are you angry with me?'

'I want us to buy a second home,' I say.

Rain comes at us on a slant, propelled by a strong breeze. It hits with a loud splatter, like dozens of transparent fingertips tapping on the windscreen.

'Don't be daft,' Stuart says.

'Why's it daft?'

'Where do you want me to start? We can't afford it . . .'

'Yes, we can. Instead of using your gran's money to pay off half our mortgage . . .'

'Lou, this is crazy! Of course we're going to pay down the mortgage, soon as the fixed term ends — why wouldn't we? We're deeper in debt than bloody . . . Greece! Manageable in the short term, but we've got to get on top of it.'

'I've seen an advert for a gated second-home community in the Culver Valley.' I don't want to tell Stuart its name, not yet. In my head, Swallowfield is already a magic word. 'It's in today's *Times*. I noticed it when we were talking to Imran. Two words jumped out at me — "peaceful" and "retreat". '

'A gated community? Have you gone mad?'

'You have an objection to gates?' I ask. *Counsel for the prosecution.* 'You've got a front door on your house, haven't you? One you lock?'

'That's different.'

'Yes, it is,' I agree. 'Just not in a way that matters.'

'Lou.' Stuart exhales endlessly. 'You don't want another house. This is nothing more than a reaction to what happened last night with Fahrenheit —'

'It doesn't need to be more. When I want food, it's a reaction to hunger. Doesn't mean I don't really need or want the food. I'm asking you to let me have something I want, Stuart. Whether I'm right to want it or not.'

'Lou, with the best will in the world, this is a want that would cost hundreds of thousands of pounds!'

'An investment,' I say, standing firm. 'You lose nothing. Long term, you stand to gain. But to be honest, I don't really care what's in it for you.'

'That much is apparent,' Stuart mutters.

'I want this. Even just thinking about it this morning has really ... lifted my heart.' In case that sounds like an empty cliché, I add, 'At a time when it badly needed lifting and nothing else was even coming close.'

Silence.

I can't bear to look at Stuart; if I saw anything but understanding I might have to pack a suitcase and leave him tonight. 'I think I deserve to be compensated for losing every other battle and conceding defeat with good grace,' I say. 'For noisy, broken nights, for my missing child –'

'Joseph's not missing! We know exactly where he is.'

'... for the threat of taped-over windows and darkness that's going to last for months. Do we?' I turn on Stuart, twisting round in my seat. 'Do we know *exactly* where Joseph is at this moment? Where is he? Tell me. I'd like to know. Is he in the boarding house common room? Playing football? Lying on his bed? Where is he?'

Stuart puts his hands on the steering wheel. Grips hard. The windows are starting to mist up. Soon we won't be able to see our escape route: we might be trapped in this car and this argument for ever. If only we'd driven all the way home while we could, and gone inside.

'This is some kind of weird displacement,' Stuart says.

'It's an investment opportunity. At least come

with me and have a look before you rule anything out.' *Who sounds hysterical now? And who sounds measured and mature?* 'This place is a residential nature reserve. Five hundred acres of stunning natural beauty – lakes, woods, fields. All kinds of rare species of birds, animals, plants.' I stop short of saying 'a fully immersive experience of nature', though I liked the sound of it when Bethan from Swallowfield's sales office said it to me on the phone. It made me realise how devoid of nature my life has been: forty-one years of living only in cities.

'There's an outdoor heated pool and a spa,' I tell Stuart. 'Twenty-four-hour security, totally safe for kids to wander about freely. No cars are allowed beyond the car park at the entrance. They have little golf-buggy-type contraptions to—'

'How do you know so much about it from glancing at an ad in the *Sunday Times*?' Stuart asks.

'I rang them.'

'When?'

'After Dr Freeman ignored my questions. Joseph was busy with his new mates. I went outside and rang the number I'd memorised from the paper.'

'Lou, this is...' Stuart breaks off, shakes his head. 'It's just some mad fantasy you've latched on to. It's absolutely crazy. We've never talked about buying a second home, never even thought about it.'

'Both those statements are false, as of today,' I point out. 'There was a picture of one of the houses in the ad – the Glass House. It was made almost entirely of glass. No shortage of natural light there.'

'Is that what this is about? The sandblasting? That won't last for ever, you know.'

'It'll last until December the fourteenth and it'll last all through Joseph's Christmas holidays,' I remind him. 'Imran said it would. I'll have three weeks with my son before school snatches him away again. I don't want to spend those three weeks in the dark recesses of a dusty house that doesn't feel like home, that I might be selling soon. And the noise – Imran's guys during the day, Mr Fahrenheit all through the night. It's . . . not a prospect I find bearable, I'm afraid.'

Stuart says nothing. He is trying to think of the definitive argument that will stop me wanting what I want. I wait for him to say that 14 December is too soon, that we'd never be in by then even if he were to agree in principle. Which he doesn't.

Not true. Bethan from Swallowfield said we could

be in by mid-November, early December if we were keen.

'Can we at least go and look?' I ask. 'We could go now — we'd be there by three if we set off now. The sales office is open till five.'

'Now? No. Definitely not.'

'Why? Shouldn't we make the most of being a spontaneous child-free couple? You haven't got any plans for the rest of the day, have you?'

'I've got work to do, Lou — lots of it.'

'Work,' I say flatly. 'Anything else?'

'Like what?' Stuart looks puzzled.

'So just work, then?' I have to check. I wouldn't want to be unfair to him.

'Yes. Work. If I'm lucky, I'll finish in time to get a reasonably early night.'

'Let's hope so,' I say innocently. 'You need your sleep.' Stuart is the sort of person who would never lay a trap, which is why he has fallen so readily into mine. *Pitiful.*

He has completely forgotten his promise to have a word with Mr Fahrenheit — this afternoon, as soon as we get back from Saviour, having taken care not to wake him too early.

3

Noise Diary – Monday 1 October, 11.10 a.m.

Last night there was more noise disturbance from
Mr Clay, for the first time ever on a Sunday night.
At about 11 p.m., just as I was on the point of
falling asleep, loud pop music started playing in his
basement. Despite it being two floors away from
my bedroom, I could hear it clearly – and by clearly
I mean the bass-line of each song pounded through
the party wall and travelled up to my room. I could
hear all the lyrics, and I could hear the distinct
voices of Mr Clay and his friends singing (or rather
screaming) along at the top of their lungs. He played

this pop music from exactly 11 p.m. until exactly
midnight, when he switched it off – literally, at
midnight on the dot.

This has never happened before – not only the
playing of music on a Sunday night, but also the
disturbance lasting precisely an hour. Mr Clay's
loud pop singalong parties are always long and
drawn out; they typically last for several hours.
I simply don't believe that on this occasion he
wanted to play music only for an hour. This was a
malicious, planned noise attack. Its sole aim was
to upset and intimidate me. In the past when I've
been round to Mr Clay's house to complain about
noise, he has stressed (in his defence) that he
only ever does this on Fridays and Saturdays: the
nights when it's acceptable to use sleep deprivation
to drive your neighbours insane, according to his
bizarre moral code. I therefore take his decision
to play loud music on a Sunday night as his way
of saying, 'You didn't appreciate how considerate I
was before and you wouldn't let me have my fun, so
let's see how you like this. From now on I'm going
to stop you from sleeping whenever I feel like it,
Sunday through Thursday, every night if I want to.'

I didn't go round to complain. Partly because my husband was against it – he thinks that, having reported the matter to the council, we must now leave it in their hands and do nothing but log all disturbances as instructed – and partly because I didn't want to give Mr Clay the satisfaction of seeing how much he'd riled me. Actually, I was more than riled; I was (and am) in a pretty bad way – the technical term would probably be 'a severely distressed state'. Does the council have any protocol for dealing with that? On previous occasions I've been very annoyed by the inconvenience, but now that Mr Clay has escalated to personal nastiness and targeted attacks, and especially given his use of boys' voices singing choral music as a weapon, I would describe myself more as distraught than angry. At about quarter past eleven last night, while Dolly Parton's '9 to 5' was booming through the wall, I was violently sick.

It wasn't food poisoning, as my husband suggested, and I am not coming down with anything. I can't prove it, but I know that what made me ill was the horrifying (and I don't use this word lightly) sensation of having my home invaded,

yet again, by a man who seeks deliberately to
harm me. I no longer feel safe here in my house.
He can torment me with his noise whenever he
wants, and there's nothing I can do to stop him. I
can't believe this is allowed to happen. If a burglar
broke in and I called the police, they would remove
him from my home immediately. Why isn't there a
law that allows people to banish, instantly, noise
that has intruded and threatened someone in their
own home? A home is meant to be a refuge from
the world, a safe haven. Mine at the moment feels
like the opposite – so much so that the only way
I can survive this ordeal, psychologically, is by
latching on to the idea of buying a second property,
somewhere far away from Justin Clay, to escape to
at weekends. I would be tempted to escape during
the week as well If it weren't for the need to stay
here near my son's school so that I can go to his
choral services three times a week.

After the music stopped at midnight, I tried to
get back to sleep. I failed. At 1 a.m., very quiet
choral music started playing: a boys' choir singing
the hymn 'O Come, O Come, Emmanuel'. The
second verse was sung by a soloist who sounded

uncannily similar to my son (and no, all choirboys do not sound the same). At one in the morning, exhausted and distressed, I'm sure I would have been paranoid enough to think, 'That's Joseph,' and be convinced that Mr Clay was using my own son's voice to torture me. The only reason I didn't think this is that I know Saviour College choir hasn't made any recordings since Joseph joined the school.

I did wonder for a chilling moment if Mr Clay had somehow illicitly made a recording of my son singing. Thankfully, I was able to reassure myself on this front: whenever Joseph has sung with the choir and it's been possible to get anywhere near him, I've been there. And Mr Clay hasn't. So it's impossible that it was Joseph's voice coming through my bedroom wall at 1 a.m. The similarity must have been a coincidence.

The hymn, like the choral music of the night before, was coming from Mr Clay's bedroom. It was loud enough to make it through the wall, though if I'd been asleep, it wouldn't have woken me. Stuart, my husband, struggled to hear it when

I woke him and asked him to listen. So ... while
I might not classify this as a noise disturbance
under normal circumstances, it is certainly a
crucial component of Mr Clay's campaign of
persecution.

After playing the hymn once, Mr Clay then didn't
play any more music. I am able to attest to this
because I was awake crying for the rest of the
night. And today I've had to phone in sick because
I'm in no fit state to go to work, thanks to my
arsehole of a neighbour. I can hardly think a
coherent sentence let alone speak one out loud,
and I look awful. I have puffy swellings and two
semicircular scabbed-over red ridges underneath
my eyes. I wouldn't want to inflict the sight of
myself on other human beings. How often is this
going to happen? One day off is one thing, but I
can't make a habit of it.

Can the council PLEASE do something, quickly,
before this man destroys my career, health and
sanity? Or before I murder him?

Noise Diary – Monday 1 October, 5.18 p.m.

This is going to be a rather unconventional noise diary entry, but I feel I need to include it for the sake of full disclosure. There would be no point in my withholding it, in any case, because Mr Clay will be sure to mention it, assuming I go through with my plan and don't chicken out. Since I was off work today and had time on my hands, I decided to do something useful, after first crashing out for three hours and catching up on sleep. I went into town and headed for Fopp on Sidney Street. In case you don't know it, Fopp is a music and DVD shop that has a split personality. It's a weird mixture of HMV-style commercial and weird beat-generation dive-cum-boutique. On one wall there's a neat display of the top twenty chart CDs, but by the counter there are piles of books about Kafka, Hunter S. Thompson, William Burroughs, Frida Kahlo. The staff always seem to have fashionably edgy hairstyles, unconventional clothes, earrings that look like rings designed for fingers except inserted into an ear lobe to create a bordered hole.

It was only because of the confused identity of the shop and its alternative-looking employees that I thought to ask the question I asked; if I'd been in HMV, I'd have managed on my own and done my best, but the baggy-eyed, indoor-hatted young man behind the counter looked as if he might be able to give me expert advice and so I thought, 'Why not?' I told him about Mr Clay. Well, I didn't mention him by name, but I said that I had a noisy neighbour who seemed intent on sabotaging my sleep every night, and that I wanted to arm myself with a means of getting my own back. I asked him which CD he would least like to be woken by at 6 a.m. Mr Clay is not an early riser. I've seen him open his bedroom curtains at ten-thirty, eleven, eleven-thirty. Certainly I've never seen him up and about earlier than ten. And once when he was telling me about a holiday he'd booked, in the days before relations were as strained as they are now, he said there was no way he was getting up before nine to catch any flight. Cruel and unusual punishment, he called it.

The man behind the counter at Fopp grinned and said, 'I've been asked that before. I always recommend the same CD: Prophecy. Capleton.' I didn't know which of those was the band and which the album title. 'I can recommend a specific track too,' he said. ' "Leave Babylon". Best song on the album. Either that or "Wings of the Morning", but "Leave Babylon"'s less conventionally tuneful – it's kind of got a dissonant sort of tune, you know? Really jarring – perfect for disturbing a neighbour. Like, the melody's there underneath, but there's, like, this kind of anti-melody overlaid on top? And they strain against each other, in a totally brilliant way? Masterpiece, it is.'

I told him my neighbour didn't deserve to have any contact with a masterpiece and asked if there wasn't an equally jarring and dissonant song he could think of that had no musical redeeming features whatsoever. He laughed. 'No, this is the right song, trust me. It's angry – you want angry, to show him you're not taking any more of his shit.' He started to sing at that point, in a put-on Jamaican accent, about equal rights, justice and revolution – an extract from 'Leave Babylon', I assumed.

It sounded impressively fierce, the way he sang it. 'All right, I'll take it,' I said. He seemed pleased

and said he'd go and find it for me. Then he
frowned and said, 'Oh, one thing I should say.
Capleton, the singer, songwriter, whatever – he's,
well, he's got some dodgy views. He's seriously
homophobic. I mean, I listen to him all the time – I
personally don't think you can boycott works of art
because their creators are dicks, but . . . it wouldn't
be fair not to tell you, in case you disagree.'

I thought about it and decided it would actually be
perfect if the artist had abhorrent views. Mr Clay
and I are at war, I explained. Why would I want
to wake him with something inoffensive when
instead I can blast the angry words of a horrible
homophobe through his bedroom wall? I want
to send as much negative energy his way as I
possibly can. The shop assistant laughed and said,
'Fair enough.'

I left Fopp feeling happier and more powerful. I
could and would do to Mr Clay exactly what he'd
been doing to me. What was to stop me? Obvious
answer: Stuart, if he was at home, but he often
wasn't. He often has to get up at four or five a.m. to
fly somewhere – those were the mornings I would

choose to execute judgement and justice according to the words of the song, I decided. In fact, I knew Stuart would be leaving home before six tomorrow morning, which was why I was keen to go to Fopp today.

As I walked home, I became obsessed by one question: why hadn't Mr Clay anticipated that I would have this idea? Did he think I was too middle class and civilised to stoop to his level and give as good as I got? Or did he not care if I fought back, because he knew what his next retaliatory move would be and knew it would totally wipe me out? Then I thought: what could his next move possibly be that would be worse than what he's doing already but not land him in serious trouble with the police? And if he did do something truly terrible, he would have no way of knowing that it wouldn't push me over the edge into doing something equally appalling in retaliation.

By the time I arrived home, I'd decided that I would take my chances. Just one song to make my point – 'Leave Babylon', only a few minutes long – and then I'd turn off the music and let him go back to sleep.

I haven't changed my mind. After what he's put me through two nights running, I'm sure even the council wouldn't begrudge me my three-minute protest. I am looking forward to it. Of course, I hope it goes without saying that if by any chance tonight is a different story and Mr Clay allows me to sleep uninterrupted, I will cancel my planned Capleton offensive.

Noise Diary – Tuesday 2 October, 3.04 a.m.

I know what he does. With the choral music, through the bedroom wall. I've worked it out. He must start by turning the volume up to the maximum setting, to create a high enough level of auditory shock to wake me from a deep sleep. Then, after maybe only a few seconds of loud, he turns it right down. By the time I realise I'm awake and that I can hear choirboys' voices, the music is playing at an acceptable volume that would be

incapable of waking anybody – that even I have to
sit quietly in order to hear. I woke Stuart when I
first heard it, half an hour ago, and I don't think
he could hear it at all this time. I say 'I don't think'
because he refused to answer when I asked him.
He snapped at me that he had to be up in about
three hours and could I please let him sleep?
Then he rolled over and was snoring again within
seconds.

I know what Justin Clay wants me to think: why
did I wake up? It's not loud. Could I be imagining
this barely audible music? Tonight there wasn't
even a prelude of obnoxious pop or country-lite.
He is trying to drive me mad, I think, in the literal
as well as the metaphorical sense. He wants me
to doubt the evidence of my ears and wonder
whether it's possible that he would wait silently
until 2.30 in the morning and then play a strange,
atonal version of the Magnificat at an inoffensive
volume. Except it was offensive at first – it must
have been. I woke in shock, my heart pounding.
I was dragged from my dream by what felt like
a sudden explosion of young boys' voices. The
only thing I can't work out is how he manages to

time it so perfectly. How does he know exactly how long the loud part has to last to wake me up? He's bound to miscalculate one day; I'll find myself fully awake before he's turned it down and I'll know for sure. Maybe I'll set up some kind of recording device – I assume the council has some of these that they loan out to the victims of noisy neighbours, in order to acquire the proof they might later need in court?

And the rich he has sent empty away. 'Has', in this version of the Mag. Not 'hath'. Did Mr Clay do any work at all yesterday, or did he devote his Monday to building his library of choral CDs to torture me with? It took me no more than an hour to walk to Fopp, buy the Capleton CD and walk home. After that, I got on with other things and even succeeded in forgetting about my war with my neighbour for a while (mainly because I was busy missing my son, but still). Now I feel stupid and naive. So I've bought one CD – so what? If I want to defeat the noise plague next door, I must be as single-minded as Justin Clay. Instead of making do with only one CD and congratulating myself on how reasonable I am because I'm only going to blast him with one song, I must set aside time to build up a library of music with which to bombard his early mornings over a period of weeks, maybe even months.

Well, there's no point in my going back to sleep now if I've got to be up at quarter to six, preparing to give Clay his alarm call. Also, the swollen patches under my eyes have split again and are simultaneously stinging and throbbing. I am in too much pain to sleep. All this crying I'm doing lately means I'm having to rub my eyes a lot, though I'm trying to avoid doing so. I hope that when you read this, council, you will take urgent action (as I've been pleading with you to do all along). It's not only my sleep and my eyes that this bastard is wrecking. At this rate my marriage won't be far behind. At the moment, I couldn't possibly hate my husband more, on account of his lack of support. I doubt I'll see things differently in the morning, since I will be as tired then as I am now. And, actually, it's already the morning.

Noise Diary – Tuesday 2 October, 12.10 p.m.

Hello, Noise Diary! Sorry – I sound like a teenager. My excuse is that I am feeling triumphant. While I don't want to tempt fate by saying anything as blatant as 'My plan worked,' or 'That went better than I could have hoped,' I must admit that my feelings at the moment are along those lines. At exactly six o'clock this morning, I pressed the 'play' button on my old ghetto blaster, having first positioned it right next to my bedroom wall, which was as close as I could get it to Justin Clay's sleeping head. Capleton's 'Leave Babylon' started to blast out (the Fopp guy was right, its melody is subtly hidden beneath a surface of cacophonous aural assault). While it played, I danced around the room, jumping up and down as heavily as I could, hoping that the pounding bass effect would be accompanied by shaking floorboards on Mr Clay's side of the party wall.

I succeeded in waking him up. When the song finished, I switched off the ghetto blaster, stopped leaping around and waited in silence. Three seconds later I heard him shout, 'All right, for fuck's sake. Point made and taken.'

I really don't want to get my hopes up (too late – they're up, and there's nothing I can do about it), and I've replayed his words over and over again in my mind, hunting for other possible interpretations, but I've found none. What he said and the way he said it sounded to me like someone unambiguously conceding defeat.

Can it really be as easy as that?

4

Pat Jervis isn't listening to me. Not looking and not listening. Instead, she's standing in front of the window, pressing the tip of her index finger against the pane.

It can't be a coincidence. Either it's a nervous tic or she has an obsession, perhaps even a fetish. Glassophilia – does such a thing exist? Last time she was here, she did exactly the same thing with the lounge mirror and the glass in one of the picture frames in the kitchen. If it were a fetish, surely she'd stroke it rather than prod it with her fingertip.

'Pat? Did you hear what I just said?'

'Oh, yes.' Still, she doesn't take her finger off the window.

'I hate myself for being so naive. I feel like tearing up my stupid noise diary –'

'Don't do that.'

I could quite easily start howling. How would Pat react? I don't think she would. I can't see her rushing over to give me a hug; it's probably against council rules, and since she can't bring herself to look at me, I'm assuming actual physical contact is out of the question.

'It's very dark in here,' Pat observes suddenly.

I stare at her. Is that all she's got to say? I didn't ring the environmental health department this morning and beg them to send someone round in order to have my house criticised.

'Funny, isn't it?' she says in a matter-of-fact tone, looking straight ahead at the reflection of the room in the window's framed blackness. 'If it were dark outside, we'd think it was light in this room with the light on. But this time of the morning, same light on – it seems dark. Because it should be light without the light.'

'It's as light as I can make it,' I say sharply. Imran's men wrapped us in cardboard and plastic yesterday afternoon, stealing all our views, sealing us in. 'At least it's not dusty yet. Next time you come, you won't be able to breathe quite so easily. They start the sandblasting tomorrow.'

Finally, Pat moves away from the window, sits in a chair opposite me. 'Next time I come? I might not need to come again. You never know your luck.' She smiles down at her bag as she pulls her notebook out of it.

I've had enough of this. 'Why are you being so non-committal all of a sudden?' I ask. 'Last time, you were all gung-ho and "Don't worry, we'll sort him out." Today you can hardly be bothered.'

'Let me tell you something you're not going to want to hear, Mrs Beeston. I've spoken to your neighbour. I didn't want to tell you until I'd heard your version of events —'

'You've spoken to him? When?'

'Today. Before I came here, I nipped next door.'

My insides clench around a hot spurt of rage, squeezing it dry. If my windows weren't covered with cardboard, I'd have known this; I'd have seen her park and go into number 19. I hate Imran, hate Pat Jervis, hate Mr Fahrenheit.

My 'version of events'. As if others might be of

equal interest and validity.

'Mr Clay admits to having disturbed you with his noise on many Friday and Saturday nights since you moved in. He admits to having played a classical CD to annoy you after the last time you went round to complain, which was the night you made your first call to our out-of-hours service – Saturday the twenty-ninth of September.'

Did she stress the word 'first', or did I imagine the emphasis? Is she subtly digging at me? I have phoned the environmental health department dozens of times this week, pleading with them to send someone round – Pat, ideally, though now that she's here and disappointing me with every word she utters, I wish I had asked for anyone but her.

If the council don't want to be telephonically stalked by people like me who grow progressively more hysterical with each call, they need to think about introducing some kind of fast-track help for sufferers of extreme neighbour noise victimisation.

'Mr Clay also admits to having played loud music again the following night, Sunday 30 September. He was still angry with you from the Saturday night, so he played his music between eleven and midnight – exactly an hour, as you said. He corroborates.'

'I don't give a toss if he corroborates or not! I've told you the truth about every aspect of the situation – whole and nothing but. I don't need his agreement.'

'I'm afraid I can't disregard his account of what's taken place,' Pat says to her notebook. 'He denies absolutely that he has ever played choral music of any kind, or anything that involves children, boys, singing. In his bedroom, with the intention of disturbing you in yours, or anywhere else in his house.'

'That's a lie. Read my diary. He's woken me up at two or three in the morning every night for the last four nights. Always with choral music, always boys – or maybe some girls too, some pieces, but definitely children, sometimes even singing the music my son sings at Saviour.'

Pat shrugs. 'That's not what Mr Clay says. He assured me he'd done nothing of the sort.'

'And you don't think someone who deliberately plays loud music to intimidate a neighbour with a valid complaint is capable of lying?' I snap.

'Oh, I have no doubt he's capable. Mrs Beeston—'

'Louise. It's bloody obvious what he's up to. He thinks that if he pleads guilty to *some* bad behaviour, he can get away with hiding the worst of what he's done – the nastier, more sinister, more insidious strand of his campaign. Look, ask Stuart if you don't believe me. He's not here now, but come round when he is and he'll tell you. It might not disturb him in the way it does me, but he's heard it several times.'

'He's your husband, though, isn't he?' says Pat.

I laugh. 'And you think that means he'd support me no matter what? Far from it. I can't...' I cut myself off in time. I was about to say, 'I can't rely on him for anything.'

'Louise. Believe me when I tell you that in my long career in environmental health, I have met every kind of noise pest on this earth. I'm not naive. I know problem neighbours lie – some a hundred per cent, others to a lesser degree. I've got a good nose for lies.' She sniffs as if to prove her point. 'But I've never come across anyone who seeks out a particular kind of music with a view to hurting a neighbour's feelings. I've never met a noisy neighbour who plays music loudly for only a few seconds, to wake someone up, then turns the

SOPHIE HANNAH

volume down just in time so that the person on the receiving end can't swear to it having been louder at first and imagines they're going crackers.'

I can't believe what I'm hearing. Cannot believe it.

Taking care to compose myself first, I say, 'All you're telling me is that you've never come across Justin Clay before. That proves nothing! I've never lived in a cardboard-swaddled, light-resistant house before – doesn't mean I'm not living in one now! Tell me this – have you ever known anyone with a noisy neighbour to grow bags under their eyes that swell up and burst?' With the index fingers of both my hands, I point at the two raw patches of skin on my face. 'And yet here I am, looking like something out of a horror film, and proving that not all people behave and react in the same way as all other people!'

Pat leans forward: eye contact at last. She squints at me. 'You need to put some St James's Balm on that – it'd clear up overnight. Trouble is, it's harder to find than the Holy Grail.' Instead of sitting back, she stays in the leaning position long after she's said her piece, long after she's stopped looking. It's as if the top half of her body has locked into a slant. She doesn't seem to have noticed that this is making it much harder for her to write in her notebook.

I want to know what she's writing. That I'm rude and aggressive? A reminder to herself to buy me the ointment she thinks I need, as a Christmas present? It could be anything.

She's mad. Must be, completely mad. That would explain everything: the change in her attitude, her noise Terminator bravado last time she was here, her lack of support now, the fingertip-pressing of random pieces of glass.

'You're evidently very upset, Louise. You've been off work how long?'

'How can I go in to work in this state?'

'I'm not accusing you of malingering. However... I'd bet good money that whatever's going on with your eyes is a psychosomatic reaction to your conflict with Mr Clay –'

'I agree.'

'– and possibly also to the upset of having your son living away from home, which you alluded to last time we spoke.'

'I didn't allude. I told you straight out.'

'Right,' she agrees. 'You did. And that's why I'm

asking you to consider if there's any chance this boys choir music you're hearing, or think you're hearing, might be . . . something else? Not real, and nothing to do with Mr Clay?'

'There is no chance,' I say. Each word is a heavy stone in my mouth that I have to spit out. 'Stuart hears it too. Unless you think we're both suffering from the same trauma-induced auditory hallucination – and I promise you, Stuart isn't distressed about anything. Apparently he isn't even worried about me looking like Frankenstein's monster. He just keeps saying, "Oh, it'll clear up."'

'Hmm.' Pat sits back, finally. 'Maybe I should talk to your husband.'

'Why, to check I'm not crazy? I'm not. The choral music is real. I don't know how you have the nerve to sit there and say these things to me! You promised you'd help me!'

'That's exactly what I'm trying to do.'

'You've got a strange way of showing it. What's stopping you from serving Mr Clay with a noise abatement order right now?'

'Mr Clay assured me that he's not going to be making a nuisance of himself in the future,' Pat says. 'Your tactic worked – you should be pleased.

After you socked it to him with a bit of loud music of your own, he drew the conclusion someone more sensible might have drawn weeks ago — he can't get away with it, not without paying a price. Oh, I've seen it countless times. It always makes me laugh. Noise offenders assume, for some reason best known to themselves, that their noise-averse neighbours wouldn't play them at their own game. Why? Well...' Pat looks up at the ceiling. 'I have a theory.'

I'm not going to ask. I don't give a shit about her theories. If she isn't going to help me, I'm not interested in anything she has to say.

'I think the mindset is along the lines of "If she can't bear loud noise then she can't use it against me because that would mean having to listen to it herself." A bit like someone who can't stand the sight of blood — they wouldn't train to be a doctor, would they?'

'That's ridiculous,' I say, wondering if she's right. 'It's loud noise you can't control that's the problem.'

'Quite. But many people are unimaginative and... well, a little bit stupid,' says Pat. 'Mr Clay strikes me as a prime example. Which is why when he told me that he wasn't going to risk making you angry again if that was how you were likely to react, I believed him.' She leans forward again, stares down at her shoes. 'I don't see him as being cunning enough to dream up a spiteful plan like the one you've described in your noise diary. I honestly don't.'

I'm too furious to speak. Furious with myself. A voice in my head is whispering: *She's right. You know she's right.*

'Louise, I think you ought to make an appointment with your doctor.'

'No! So what if he's unimaginative? He's got friends, hasn't he? A girlfriend? Anyone could have suggested the choral music to him – who says it was his idea?' Too late, I realise she might only have meant my eyes: that I should see a doctor to sort out the skin eruptions.

'Where are you going?' Pat asks out of the blue.

'What?'

She points at the car keys I'm clutching. 'You said when I arrived that you were on your way out.'

'Oh. I . . . just . . .' I don't want to tell her. I don't have to. It's none of her business.

'I hope you're not planning a long drive,' she says. 'You don't look anywhere near well enough.'

'I'm going to the Culver Valley. For a sales tour of a second-homes development. I'm thinking of buying a place there. So that I get can away from here, at least at weekends.'

Holidays will be trickier, because Stuart won't always be able to take the time off work. It won't be a problem for me, thankfully; as soon as I heard that Joseph had got a place at Saviour, I reorganised my work schedule so that I could work longer days in the office during term time and from home during school holidays, when I would also take all my annual leave. I didn't think work would agree, and was planning to resign if they didn't, but to my surprise they said it was fine.

The tricky part will be confessing that my plan is for Joseph and me to live at Swallowfield whenever he's not at school, even if that means leaving Stuart behind in Cambridge, as it often will.

Am I trying to stealth-leave my husband, subtly and by degrees? Trying to make a point by insisting on taking Joseph as far away from Saviour as I can, whenever I can, just to prove to Dr Freeman that I'm in charge?

Whatever my motivation is for wanting to leave Cambridge, I would prefer not to know. It's as if

I'm receiving my instructions from an authority that has nothing to do with me and isn't even part of me – one I trust absolutely. I know what I need to do and that's enough. It's a weird feeling. Like none I've ever had before.

I need to buy a house on Swallowfield Estate.

'I'd advise against,' says Pat. For a minute, I forgot she was there.

'Sorry?'

'Now's not a good time to be making important decisions, Louise. Trust me. It sounds to me like you're trying to run away. What you should be doing's sorting things out here – at home.'

'Excuse me?' I laugh. 'First, I *did* trust you, to a ridiculous degree, and look where it got me – you believe my neighbour's lies over me. Second, who are you to tell me how to arrange my life? I don't even know you. You know nothing about me.'

'I know you shouldn't drive to the Culver Valley. Don't do it, Louise.'

The room has darkened, as if someone has adjusted the dimmer switch, but that's impossible. Pat and I are the only people here. Shaking, I haul myself to my feet and say, 'I'd like you to leave now, please.'

Pat stands too. 'Stay here,' she says, looking past my shoulder, at the wall behind me. 'Get some sleep. Forget buying a second home. The noise will stop. It already has. Mr Clay won't bother you again. Please take my advice.'

'That's not true! You've not listened to anything I've said. Look, just ... go.'

She nods, apparently unoffended, and begins to rock her way to the door, tilting from side to side as she goes.

'Ring me if you need me. You know where I am,' she says before leaving. 'And keep writing the diary.'

5

It is like falling in love. It *is* falling in love. I knew
it was going to be. I knew Swallowfield would be
the right place. Two hours ago, as I drove past the
sign that says 'Welcome to the Culver Valley', I
imagined myself doing the journey with Joseph, his
happy voice asking, 'How much longer?' from the
back seat. He'll be beside himself with excitement
whenever we come here, desperate to get out of the
city and back to his other house in the beautiful
countryside outside Spilling.

Of course, I didn't know for sure, on my way to
Swallowfield, that I'd want to buy: this is what I tell
myself and, although it doesn't feel true, it must be.

I hadn't seen the estate yet, or any of the houses. I hadn't been on Bethan's sales tour. All I knew was that I felt drawn, as if by a magnet, and couldn't resist. Didn't want to resist.

As I drove along the approach road to Swallowfield, I imagined that it might have been rolled out, brand new and only seconds ago, for my sole use. There were no other cars on it going in either direction. I lowered my window to see if I could hear traffic in the distance; I couldn't. The only sound, apart from my car's engine, was that of the birds — so many and so varied that it made me realise I'd never really heard or listened to anything like it before. People say birds chirp — they call it 'song' — but I heard no tunes and all kinds of other strange utterances, most of which couldn't be summed up so easily. It was like listening to an uncoordinated orchestra playing above my head, one that contained dozens of different instruments.

When I saw, coming up on the left, the large pale green sign with 'Swallowfield' printed across it in lower-case white letters, I had a crazy idea. I was a little early for my meeting with Bethan Lyons, the sales director, so I decided to try something that, in Cambridge, would be regarded as a suicide attempt:

I slowed down, drove into the middle of the road and parked horizontally across the white line that separates eastbound traffic from westbound.

Nothing bad happened. No other cars came. I wasn't worried that they would, either. I felt utterly calm and at peace, as though nothing could happen here that would threaten my safety or happiness in any way. It was the oddest feeling. I opened the car door and looked to my right at the fields, hedges and trees — at the hills in the distance with white and pastel-coloured cottages, warm beige stone farmhouses and black-painted barns dotted across them — and I almost closed my eyes and fell asleep on the spot. Finally, I could relax. I was home. (Technically, the opposite was the case, but I didn't, and don't, and never have cared about facts when they don't feel true.)

It was cold — and still is — but the sun was shining brightly, lighting up patches of vivid green everywhere I looked. It was as if I'd strayed into some kind of magical other-world, a sparkling alternative reality that most people knew nothing about. And this was before I'd set foot on the estate itself. I don't know how I'd have dealt with the disappointment if Swallowfield had turned out to be hideous. All I can say (and Stuart won't believe me, unless he feels the same way himself, which he won't) is that I knew it wouldn't happen. I knew Swallowfield would exceed my expectations.

'So, the nature-only part of the estate starts here,' Bethan says, bringing me back to the moment. We have been round the stunning glass sculpture of a show home, the café and the shop, and now we are in the official crested Swallowfield Range Rover, about to go through wooden gates, off the gravelled lane and on to a wide grassy path that has a lake to one side of it. Swallowfield has five lakes, and residents are allowed to swim and fish in all but one of them. Three of them, the smallest, have houses around them and still a few bare plots for new houses to be built, and the two largest lakes are in the purely rural bit that Bethan is driving me around now, on the land that will never be developed, Swallowfield's residents' own private cultivated wilderness. I want it for myself, and for Joseph, with a desperation that verges on hysteria, though Bethan wouldn't be able to guess from looking at me. I stare out of the Range Rover's window at the ripples on the surface of the water and the wooden jetty, and I can see Joseph throwing off his clothes and diving in on a stifling hot day. I picture myself leaping in after him, Stuart shouting after us, 'Rather you than me! I'll save my swimming for the spa, thank you very much.'

I can't wait to see the spa. Bethan says I can have a swim and a complimentary half-hour back, neck and shoulder massage. Well, it's only complimentary if I end up buying a house here, but I already know that I will. I made up my mind for certain when Bethan buzzed me in and I drove through the gates on to the estate; my feeling of 'This is right, this is the one and only right thing in my life' intensified, and has been intensifying ever since.

'So, this is the rural idyll bit,' Bethan says, laughing. She has an odd habit of looking in her rear-view mirror every time she addresses me, as if she's talking to someone sitting in the back instead of beside her in the front passenger seat, as I am.

Maybe she doesn't understand that I would only be able to see her eyes in the mirror if she could see mine. I think about Pat touching the mirror in my lounge with her index finger...

Am I such a frightful sight at the moment that anybody would prefer to look at their own reflection than at me? Actually, I wouldn't blame

Bethan if she felt that way, even if the skin beneath my eyes weren't such a mess; she's got thick shoulder-length hair the colour of dark honey, big brown eyes, perfectly straight teeth, flawless skin. Her only not-ideal features, if I'm being strict, are too-thin lips and a too-small nose that looks sharp, even though it wouldn't be if you touched it. In spite of these minor physical blemishes, ninety-nine out of a hundred men would choose her over me, I'm sure.

'Honestly, it sounds silly, but it *is* an idyll, this part of the estate,' she gushes. 'It's the heart and soul of Swallowfield, really – that's what all our home-owners say. This is where you and your family will come when you want a purely rural experience – no houses, no car noise, hardly any people – you might bump into one or two walkers or picnickers, but most of our residents tell us they never bump into anyone out here. And no one who isn't a resident can get in, obviously, so you'll have five hundred acres of beautiful countryside all to yourself.'

'Wow,' I breathe. 'It's like paradise, it really is.' Privately, I am thinking, 'All to myself apart from having to share it with all the other homeowners, and there are at least fifty houses here.' I don't care;

if anything could put me off, it certainly isn't that. Stuart and I could buy a holiday home that we wouldn't have to share with anyone, but it wouldn't have 500 acres attached to it, or an award-winning £10-million spa, or a helipad (not that we'll ever need it) or a concierge service, whatever that is. No doubt I will find out.

It must be satisfying to be Bethan, I think to myself, especially when the person she's trying to sell to is me. I'm a sure thing. She is peddling desire to someone who is already head over heels, and I can't imagine that anyone would come here and not be instantly smitten. Bethan's job-satisfaction levels must be sky high.

'Unlike a lot of gated second-home communities, we don't allow subletting or holiday rentals,' she tells me, 'so the only other people you'll ever see anywhere on the estate are the staff and other residents. Our homeowners love the exclusivity of Swallowfield.' She laughs. 'To be honest, they love everything about it – the beauty, the incredibly fresh air, the quiet, the absolute safety. We're gated, obviously, and there's a discreet but constant security presence, so from a lock-up-and-leave point of view, you won't find better, and the best thing is that it's totally safe for children to roam around unsupervised, and where else is that possible? Not even in a village these days. Course, the other thing with a village is that people resent you, don't they? City folk buying up the houses to use as second homes — here you don't get any of that because it's a community where it's *everyone's* second home. And what everyone forgets about villages is that they can be incredibly noisy — all that agricultural machinery, farmworkers going about their daily business. There's none of that here.'

Her use of the word 'noisy' has unsettled me. There might be no agricultural machinery at Swallowfield, but there are other people. What's to stop Mr Fahrenheit buying a second home here? Or someone like him?

'And all the amazing animal and plant life we've got!' Bethan goes on. 'Fascinating though many of our homeowners are, they're unlikely to be your most interesting neighbours — there's all kinds of rare species living here. You'll be amazed by what you see when you nip out for a walk — rabbits, deer, dragonflies, frogs, all different kinds of birds. And almost the best thing of all is watching the changing of the seasons at

Swallowfield. You just don't notice it in a city in the same way, but here . . . oh!' She half closes her eyes, as if in ecstasy. She is overdoing it, but I don't mind.

'You said the homeowners love the quiet. Is it always quiet here?'

Bethan giggles. 'So much so, it'll freak you out.'

Good. And no, it won't.

'Most of our homeowners are city dwellers like yourself, and *so* many say they find it spooky at first, the silence. You hear birds and animals and, apart from that, nothing.'

We have driven nearly all the way round the lake on the way to another one that looks even bigger. 'What's that little wooden building?' I ask. 'Is that for the security staff?'

'No, that's a bird hide. That's where you'll come with your son – how old did you say he was?'

'Seven.'

'Perfect age,' Bethan says, making me wonder what's wrong with six and eight. 'What's his name?'

'Joseph.'

'That's a beautiful name. And it won't matter here that he's an only child – he won't be lonely, I can assure you.'

I do an internal double take. What an extraordinarily tactless thing to say. For all Bethan knows, Stuart and I desperately wanted more children and couldn't have them.

It doesn't matter anywhere that Joseph's an only child, I want to say but don't. It only matters that Dr Freeman has stolen him.

'You can bring Joe here in the evening and watch all the birds, try and catch a glimpse of the beavers.' Bethan turns to face me, briefly, before looking back at the track ahead. 'Swallowfield's what childhood ought to be,' she says. 'Parents let their kids wander out of the house without even saying where they're going or when they'll be back. I bet you can't believe you'll ever be willing to do that, but I promise you, once you get used to life here, you will.'

Joe? For a second, I almost say, 'Who's that?' We've never called him Joe.

'It's unimaginable in the city, but here children head off into the woods, meet up with friends at the trampolines or by the climbing frame – we've got an amazing playground, I'll show you on the way out—'

'I'm just thinking about noise,' I say, interrupting her. Rude, no doubt, but I can't help it.

'I told you, there is no noise.'

'Yes, but . . . let's say I were to buy a house and the person in the house next door starts to play his stereo too loud –'

'Ah!' says Bethan knowingly. 'I see what you're driving at. You've no need to worry, honestly. Ensuring that Swallowfield is peaceful and quiet at all times is our number one priority. All our homeowners come here to escape from the noise that you just can't get away from in a city, so we take it very seriously indeed. No one's allowed to make any noise, at any time of day or night, that disturbs anybody else. It's in the lease that everyone signs. We've not needed to yet, but, believe me, we'd be rigorous about enforcing it if we had to. If you're ever sitting on your balcony or on your terrace, or inside your house, and you're disturbed by the sound of anyone's television, or even a too-loud conversation, you'll just give Bob a ring and he'll deal with it straight away. There was an incident last year – one of our homeowners had a hen party in her house. The noise was audible to the house next door, who rang Bob, who was straight in his van and driving round to the hen-night house to very politely remind the lady of the rule about absolute peace and quiet. She was mortified and switched the music off straight away. That's quite honestly the only noise issue we've had in the seven years Swallowfield has existed. And I promise you, everybody here – everybody – cares as much about preserving the tranquillity as you do.'

I doubt it. What about the hen-night woman? Why did she need Bob to mortify her before she realised that her music was too loud and might annoy people?

'We don't even play music in the gym or at the swimming pool,' says Bethan. 'The spa rules are very strict about noise. If children shout and scream in or by the pool, they're asked to get out. Jumping in isn't allowed – that's a new rule since last year. Some of the homeowners complained about children jumping in and making loud splashing noises while they were trying to have a quiet, relaxing swim.'

I smile. These are the kinds of neighbours I want to have: ones who regard a loud splash as unreasonable and are not willing to put up with it. I will have to explain to Joseph that he must enter the swimming pool silently, via the steps. He won't mind.

'Similarly, the rural parts of the estate. If you

and your family go out into one of the fields for a picnic and you happen to bump into a homeowner who's having a little disco, making a bit of a racket – not that that would *ever* happen – give Bob a ring and he or one of his men'll be straight round. If children are shrieking as they leap into the lake, call Bob. Not allowed. That's in the lease too, at the insistence of certain homeowners.'

All right, now I'm impressed. No noise allowed, even in the wilderness. Have I found, by some miracle, somewhere I can live and be the least-obsessed-with-noise member of the community? The idea makes me want to explode with joy.

'Of course, it's something you'll need to think about before you sign on the dotted line,' says Bethan, as we drive through what looks like a river into a field bordered on two sides by tall evergreen trees. 'Source of the River Culver – right here in Swallowfield,' she tells me as an aside.

'What will I need to think about?'

'The requirement not to make noise. I mean, obviously you're not expected to glide silently from your house to the spa – the normal sounds of everyday life are fine, but we do expect homeowners to keep in mind that Swallowfield is a tranquil haven for all of us, so to keep noise to a minimum. So, if you're on your way from your house to the spa or the shop and you're chatting to your husband or Joe, do it with consideration for others rather than at the tops of your voices — that's all we ask — so that if someone's coming along in the opposite direction and seems to be lost in their own thoughts, you won't intrude on their peace of mind.'

I can't wait any longer. I need to live here, as soon and as much as I can. 'You said on the phone that I could buy and be in within a couple of months. Can a house be built that quickly?'

'Oh — no, I meant if you bought one of our resales and if you were a cash buyer you could maybe be in that quickly. But if you want to buy a plot of land and have a bespoke—'

'A resale's fine,' I say, not knowing what one is. I assume the clue is in the name: houses that were bespoke built for other homeowners who now want to sell. 'How many do you have available? Vacant possession, ideally. Or someone who can move out quickly.'

Bethan laughs. 'Wow, you're keen, aren't you? Are you sure you don't want to go the bespoke route? Most people who buy here—'

'I need to be in by the fourteenth of December at the latest,' I tell her. 'That's when my son breaks up for the Christmas holidays. I want to pick him up from school and drive him straight here.'

'Oh... well, yes, then a resale it's going to have to be.' I hear the enthusiasm in her voice dip, and the way she then tries to resurrect it artificially. Less money for Swallowfield with a resale, presumably; less commission for her. 'We've got three at the moment. If you like, we can go back to the sales office now and—'

'Are any of them all glass, like the show home? Or anything like the show home?'

'Two of them are actually barn-style homes, so, no – wooden, not glass. The third has a whole wall of glass at the front, covering all three storeys, so it's completely glass-fronted.'

That's the one I'm buying.

'It's a lovely light house – perfect for a tidy family, I'd say!'

'Tidy?' I wasn't expecting that. I can't think what she might mean.

'The Boundary – that's its name – overlooks Topping Lake. If you buy it and your living room or your bedroom's messy, it'll be seen by swimmers in the summer, and sailors out on their boats, and paddle-boarders.'

'Oh, I see. That won't be a problem. I'm pretty tidy. My husband and son aren't, but...'

I break off. Does Bethan honestly imagine I would care what another Swallowfield resident in a passing canoe thought about the state of my house? I wonder if this is her subtle way of telling me that the lease has issues with domestic disorder as well as noise. I wouldn't be altogether surprised; homeowners who complain about splashing noises in swimming pools might well object equally to the sight of a dishevelled duvet as they sail on the lake.

The Boundary. Topping Lake. That is my house, my new address.

'Can I look at The Boundary today? Now?' I ask Bethan.

6

Noise Diary – Friday 12 October, 9.20 a.m.

We have entered a new phase. Last night, for the first time since my noise war with Justin Clay started, my husband was away overnight. Which Mr Clay knew, because when Stuart's at home his car is parked in one of the residents' bays on the street rather than in Stansted airport's short-stay or long-stay car park.

I couldn't sleep. Not that I've been sleeping particularly well since all this unpleasantness began, and since the house has been full of builders' dust. Predictably, I have turned out to be far more sensitive to the dust than Stuart, who it seems is not very sensitive to anything. Most nights I find myself waking four or five times, either needing to cough or jerking to attention in a panic after dreaming that Mr Clay is playing choral music. Which, recently, he hasn't been. Having told Pat Jervis he'd never done it in the first place, I knew he would stop completely for a while to make me wonder if he might have been telling the truth – if Pat could be right and I'd imagined the boys' voices coming through my bedroom wall.

I understand Mr Clay's psychology better now than I did before. He's not a little bit stupid, as Pat said. He might present as crass and dense when he's coasting along happily on autopilot, but lurking somewhere beneath the cannabis-fugged surface of his brain is a shrewd strategic sensibility that he is able to access when he applies himself. And, despite the current poor state of my own exhaustion-eroded mind, I am obviously capable of similarly astute calculation, because I knew he would choose last night for his first attack in a while. That's why I couldn't sleep. Well, to be

more accurate, I decided not to sleep. I sat in bed
and waited. I thought about the expression 'going
to the mattresses'. I first heard it in *The Godfather*
movie and it stuck in my mind. It means preparing
for war: moving out of your house, going to hide in
a warehouse with nothing but mattresses to make
it more comfortable. Not an exact analogy with my
situation, but close enough.

I wanted to prove or disprove my own theory, to
try to catch Mr Clay's few seconds of loud music
designed to make sure I wake up before he turns
the volume down to audible-but-inoffensive. That
was the only thing I turned out to be wrong about
This time he went for full-on loud Two In the
morning, a boys' choir blasting out 'King of Glory,
King of Peace'. Of course, I should have anticipated
this too. There was no need for Mr Clay to bother
with the quiet phase last night, since there was no
possibility of engineering a row between me and
Stuart: 'But it's so quiet, you can hardly object.' / 'I
don't care how quiet it is, it's still the middle of the
night and he's only doing it to hurt me.'

I think this is what Mr Clay intends to do from now

on: persecute me when I'm alone and he knows I won't be able to prove anything.

Except I will. I can buy some kind of recording device. (God knows where from. I haven't owned one since the tape recorder I had in the 1980s. I don't know what people use to record things these days. Maybe I'll ask the man in Fopp.) What I need is a machine that can record sound and also log the time and date that the sound was recorded. Though how would I prove the sound was coming from Mr Clay's house and not my own? His obvious defence would be to allege that I was so vindictive and obsessed with punishing him that I was trying to frame him – creating noise myself in order to blame it on him.

It shouldn't be too hard to distract him somehow and then sneak some impartial witnesses into my house the next time Stuart's away. I'm sure I can think of something. A surprise phone call to Mr Clay; a staged fight between students at the back of our houses (whom I would pay handsomely, of course) involving lots of swearing and threats of violence. While Mr Clay hurried to one of his back windows to see what was going on, I could let my witnesses in at the front. They'd have to be people who wouldn't mind staying up all night. I'd need to pay them too, probably.

Maybe Pat Jervis would agree to be the visiting nocturnal witness? She might be fickle in her loyalties, but my sense is that she's someone who likes a challenge. If I said to her, 'Do this one thing, and you'll see I'm right. If I'm not, I'll accept that you're right and I'm going crazy.' Or maybe it would be easier to ask one of her colleagues, Trevor Chibnall or Doug Minns, who would be less likely to try and interfere in the rest of my life.

(This is a side issue, but it's totally out of order for a council environmental health officer to tell someone she's visiting in a professional capacity not to run away from a problem by buying a holiday home in the Culver Valley. I still cannot believe Pat Jervis said that to me with a straight face. Even hospital staff, in real life, don't intrude in that way, despite the misleading impression given by TV shows like *House* and *Casualty* in which surgeons say, 'While I remove your appendix, let's discuss

your fear of romantic commitment.' In spite of
the inappropriate discouragement I received, I am
buying a second home in the Culver Valley – it's all
going through at the moment. Not that it's any of
Pat's business.)

Whatever plans I make, they need to be beyond Mr
Clay's imaginative capacity, since he will be trying
to second-guess me at every stage. I need to think
about this more when I'm not so tired.

Noise Diary – Thursday 18 October, 11 a.m.

I don't have much energy for writing today, so
I'll keep this as brief as possible. I'm not sure
there's much point in my continuing with this diary
anyway, since I'm unlikely to be believed. I have no
proof, and it would sound insane if I told anyone.
Because it is; Mr Clay must be quite, quite mad to
be doing what he's doing to me.

This can't only be about noise – his right to make
it, my complaints about it. Perhaps that was the

catalyst, but the seeds of his aptitude for the kind
of sustained, escalating vindictiveness he is now
displaying must have been sown in his personality
long before he met me. I know nothing about his
background or childhood. Maybe he was the victim
of a heinous wrong that planted a fountain of anger
and vengefulness in his heart that's been spouting
ever since. Maybe he was too scared of the person
or people who injured him to do anything about it,
and that's why he needs to get stoned all the time,
to numb his rage. And then I entered his life, with
my unwillingness to let his fun disrupt my nights,
and suddenly his suppressed acrimony started to
froth and bubble until it spilled out all over me – a
polite, law-abiding woman he's not at all afraid of; a
convenient proxy target.

I can't prove that any of that's true either.

Anyhow, the bald facts are as follows: Stuart is
away again, and Mr Clay has taken his campaign
to a new level. Last night, I spent the evening in
the lounge watching television. There was nothing
good on, but I hate being alone in the house and
I'd rather have the TV on than off, if only to hear

the sound of human voices. (Pathetic, I know. But if I sat in silence, I might start to think about how much easier it is for Stuart to cope with Joseph's absence during term time than it is for me, because he's away quite regularly himself. I might then start to wonder if this has occurred to Stuart at any point. He hasn't mentioned it, if it has. Before too long, I might be roaming the dark streets of Cambridge screaming, 'Where is my superior second husband?' All of that sounds like something worth avoiding, so I watch television instead.)

At about ten-thirty I turned off the TV and the lounge light, and was about to go upstairs to bed when I heard boys singing. This time it was 'Lift Thine Eyes', and it wasn't coming through any part of the wall my house shares with Mr Clay's. It was coming from outside. I wasn't sure at first, so I walked over to the window. As I got closer, my doubts evaporated; the voices were directly outside my lounge, on the street. The only thing separating me from them was a pane of glass and Imran's cardboard, scaffolding and plastic sheeting.

At first I was pleased. If Mr Clay was standing on the pavement with his ghetto blaster, I thought, then someone apart from me would hear it: one of our other neighbours, or a passer-by. If I could find even one person to back me up then I could prove to Pat Jervis that I was genuinely the victim of a hate crusade. I wondered if Clay was finally losing his grip – if he was so puffed up with venom that he'd forgotten about plausible deniability, which originally was the lynchpin of his campaign. Was the temptation of my wrapped-up house, which from the outside looks like a Christo and Jeanne-Claude artwork (if that means anything to you, Cambridge Council – if not, they're sculptors whose USP is that they wrap things up, big things like the Pont Neuf bridge), too much for him to resist? Perhaps he decided it was worth the risk of revealing himself to our neighbours in order to experience the intense joy of pure, undiluted victory, however fleeting. He knew I couldn't run to the window and catch him at it because my view is blocked by cardboard and plastic.

I ran to the front door instead, but by the time I got there and opened it, he and the music were gone.

As I knew they would be. A man in a checked flat cap was walking his dog along the pavement and had almost reached the corner of Weldon Road, where it meets Hills Road. 'Excuse me!' I called to him. He came back. I asked him if he'd heard the music and seen a man with some kind of device for playing it. He said he hadn't. He must have been lying. There's simply no way he could have been where he was, having walked past my house when he must have, and not heard it.

A friend of Mr Clay's, strategically placed to impersonate an innocent bystander, and torment me still further? I put my coat on, went out and rang number 15's bell, to see if they'd heard anything, but their house was in darkness and no one came to the door.

Noise Diary – Friday 19 October, 10.54 p.m.

I don't know how he's doing it. Is it possible that the whole street is in league with him against me? Tonight he didn't wait till I turned off the TV and

the light. He started to play choral music outside
the lounge window while I was watching, or trying
to watch, *EastEnders*. He must have had the
volume up as high as it would go. What equipment
is he using? Some kind of boom box – a relic from
the break-dancing-on-street-corners era? Does
he have some cunning way of angling the speakers
so that the sound pours into my house but not
out into the street? I wonder if he's pulled back
Imran's plastic sheeting and set down the ghetto
blaster on the horizontal wooden platform inside
the scaffolding, but even if he has, the noise would
still spill out on to the street. And yet no one heard
it, no one but me.

Tonight it was another hymn: 'Dear Lord and
Father of Mankind'. I was nearly sick when I heard
the first notes and realised which song it was.
Saviour's choir sang it at the first Choral Evensong
Stuart and I attended after Joseph started school
in September. It was the first hymn I heard my son
sing with his choir. I started to cry as I listened,
because it sounded so beautiful and Joseph was
part of that, and yet I was so unhappy; I felt as if my
heart was cracking into ever smaller pieces. Every

note strained my soul nearly to breaking point, like
a heavy boot leaning its full weight on cracking ice.
I used to love 'Dear Lord and Father of Mankind'
– it was my favourite hymn – but since that first
Choral Evensong I haven't been able to think about
it and would take steps to avoid hearing it again.
Strangely, I don't feel that way about any other
piece I've heard Joseph sing with the choir. I don't
know why. Perhaps because 'Dear Lord and Father
of Mankind' was the first, or because it meant
more to me than any other hymn – but how could
Mr Clay have known this? I don't believe it can be a
coincidence that he chose that song.

At first, when I heard it playing outside the lounge,
I was too horrified to move. Then I stood up and,
foolishly, ran to the window. It's pathetic that even
after so many days with no natural light, this is my
automatic response when I hear a noise from the
street. You'd think that by now my brain would be
subliminally aware that I need to head for the front
door instead.

Predictably, the window showed me nothing but
blackness and the reflection of my lounge – of

myself in it, wild-haired with scabbed-up puffy
eyes, wearing old pyjamas that, after several days,
aren't particularly clean or fragrant. It's ironic that
I've spent so much more time in my pyjamas since
I've been unable to sleep properly. I pretty much
only get dressed now to go to Saviour to hear
Joseph sing.

I turned and was on my way to the front door to
try to catch Mr Clay in the act – the music was still
playing – when something made me turn back.
I don't know what it was; something to do with
what I'd seen reflected in the window, I think. I
moved closer to the glass and looked again. There
was nothing unusual or unexpected about what I
saw: a sofa, two chairs, a lamp, a coffee table, two
alcoves containing messy shelves with too many
books crammed into them. Just my lounge, with
me in it. Yet something about what I was looking at
was making my heart beat dangerously fast, and a
tiny voice inside me was warning me to turn away
before I saw something I wouldn't be able to bear.
I had to get out of the room as quickly as I could,
so I ran out into the hall, then had to lean against
the wall for a few seconds to get my breath back.

I decided there would be plenty of time later to wonder what disturbing thing I might have noticed that wasn't immediately obvious when I looked again, whereas I might only have seconds to catch Mr Clay, so I got to the front door as quickly as I could and threw it open.

Nothing. No sound, nobody on the street. Not even a passer-by. This time I knew beyond doubt that what seemed to be the case simply couldn't be: it was physically impossible. Seconds earlier, 'Dear Lord and Father of Mankind' had been playing. Mr Clay couldn't have switched it off and got himself off Weldon Road and back inside his house so quickly.

I had an idea: maybe he'd left some kind of hi-tech music system on the pavement, then gone back to his house and controlled it remotely, from inside number 19. If so, he could have pressed 'Stop' at the exact moment that he saw my door open. I ran outside and looked: nothing. No ghetto blaster. No machine of any sort.

How did he do it, then? Could he have done it without a machine on the street? Maybe he broke into my house yesterday while Stuart was away and I was out at Choral Evensong. He could have implanted some kind of invisible or well-concealed speakers in my lounge, somewhere near the window. Under the floorboards perhaps.

I took the lounge apart (and am too shattered, for the time being, to put it back together again) and found nothing. I concluded that it was more likely that Mr Clay had devised some way to project music into the night – maybe he opened his lounge window and balanced a speaker on the sill, angled so that the sound was aimed directly at the pavement outside my house . . . That strikes me as feasible.

One thing seemed to me to be certain: someone else must have heard a hymn played that loud. I brushed my teeth and my hair and went outside again. There were ground-floor lights on in three houses apart from mine: Mr Clay's, number 16 and number 12. I decided to try number 16, since it's directly opposite. The man who lives there alone, Philip Darrock-Jones, is a relatively famous musical conductor who has worked with all the major British orchestras and many international ones too.

I like Philip. He has lived on Weldon Road for more than twenty years, he once told me, and, unlike most of the privacy-obsessed newer residents who install shutters or opaque glass in all their windows the instant they move in, he never even bothers to draw his lounge curtains, despite having what are very obviously rare and valuable paintings all over his walls. Being as left-wing as he is, he probably feels morally obliged to share his art collection with passers-by who can't afford to buy original art themselves. I follow him on Twitter, so I know, for example, that he would very much like to be forced to pay more tax than he does at the moment. He doesn't seem unduly worried about people like me and Stuart who don't want to but would have to if he had his way, but despite disagreeing with him about this, I can't help thinking that the altruism that is so obviously behind his opinions is quite sweet. I also like him because he annoys Mr Clay, who strongly objects to the 'Vote Labour' poster that is on permanent display in Philip's bedroom window,

even when there is no election in sight; I've heard
Clay complain to his girlfriend Angie that the
poster lowers the tone, makes the street look
scruffy and studenty, and brings down the whole
neighbourhood: the same view Stuart holds about
houses with pollution-blackened brickwork. For
all I know, Philip Darrock-Jones's idea of tone-
lowering might be lounging on your sofa, in full
view of anyone who walks past, inhaling marijuana
smoke through a plastic bottle with a hole burned
at one end of it. These things are all relative.

Philip came to the door when I knocked, and
seemed genuinely pleased to see me. If he noticed
that I was wearing pyjamas under my coat he
showed no sign of it. I had to fight quite hard not
to be dragged in for a cup of coffee, but eventually
I managed to convince him I didn't have enough
time. I told him I just wanted to ask a quick
question: had he heard a boys' choir singing about
twenty minutes ago? Was he in his lounge then?
Had he seen anyone on the street, since he never
closed his curtains? He frowned. No, he hadn't, he
said. He'd heard nothing, seen nothing, and he'd
been in the lounge the whole time.

I nearly fell down in a heap on his doorstep. I'd
been frightened of him saying what he said,
because I knew I would believe him if he did. Philip
wouldn't lie to me. If 'Dear Lord and Father of
Mankind' were blaring out at top volume outside
his house, he would notice it more than any other
neighbour, being a music man.

I must have turned pale or looked shaky,
because Philip asked me if I was all right and
tried again to get me over his threshold with
offers of recuperative brandy. He asked me what
was wrong and why I was asking about a boys'
choir. I had the weirdest physical sensation: as
if someone was drawing, very gently, all the
arteries, veins, nerves and muscles out of my
body, leaving me empty and floppy, without
substance. I shook my head and said it didn't
matter. If my own husband doesn't believe me – if
Pat Jervis, whose life's work is to defeat noise
vandals, doesn't believe me – why should Philip,
who believes that people are fundamentally
nice and all want to look after each other? I can
imagine him furrowing his capacious brow and
asking, 'But why on earth would Mr Clay want

to be so nasty to you?' and I couldn't have held
myself together if he'd said that.

Philip was certain there was no music playing on
the street twenty minutes earlier. He was an eye-
and ear-witness to the absence of boys' voices
singing. I wouldn't have been able to convince him
that he was wrong and I was right.

I didn't bother asking any of the other neighbours.
Once again, I realised, I'd underestimated Mr Clay.
Of course he wouldn't play empirically verifiable
loud music in the street. He wouldn't be so stupid.

So. Hidden speakers in my lounge. It's the only
explanation.

After I got back from Philip's, I locked the door,
went to the kitchen and took the little packet of
cannabis out of the drawer. From another drawer, I
pulled out a box of matches, and from the counter
I picked up a half-empty bottle of mineral water.
I took all three to the lounge and sat down on the
sofa, thinking, 'I am going to take some drugs.
Maybe if I get high like Mr Fahrenheit (that's what

I call Mr Clay) I will be able to access his mindset more easily – the druggie wavelength; I will be able to look around this room and intuitively know where he's planted the invisible speakers.'

I didn't go through with my plan to get high. I remembered that Mr Fahrenheit, when I saw him do this, had a piece of what looked like silver foil stretched over the top of the bottle. I couldn't be bothered to go back to the kitchen for foil, so I stayed where I was and cried instead.

At this rate, if no one helps me to prove what's going on and put a stop to it, my next-door neighbour is going to kill me.

TWO

December

7

'Mum, look how high I'm going!' Joseph yells at me, bouncing up and down on the trampoline. He's with a friend who, so far, has jumped silently, as I'm sure his watching mother must be smugly aware.

'Ssssh!' I hiss, running over just in case I need to tell Joseph again because he didn't hear me the first time. As I move towards him, I glance to my left at the hard-surfaced tennis court, on which a young blond married couple, protected from the cold by tracksuits and fleeces with hooded tops, are playing half-heartedly and laughing at their own uselessness. I met them at the spa last week and we talked for a bit — everyone seems keen to chat to the new homeowners, probably so that they can gossip about us later – but I can't remember their names. Hers was something unusual like Melody or Carmody, but not either of those.

Only about one in five of their shots makes it over the net. As I move towards the trampoline, I watch them to see if they are going to react at all to Joseph's enthusiastic outburst or to my 'Ssssh!', but they don't seem interested. They are too caught up in their own giggling, which isn't much quieter than the noise I made, and is going on for longer. The mother of the other boy on the trampoline doesn't seem concerned about the breach of the peace either. And Joseph is already mouthing, 'Sorry, Mum! I forgot!'

We moved into The Boundary less than a week ago, but I am already starting to work out the unwritten rules. It isn't noise that people worry about so much as noise that no one is taking steps to deal with. My 'Ssssh!' would have reassured everyone in the vicinity that I was aware of the problem and would sort it out, and that is all people want here: the comfort of knowing that their neighbours value quiet and tranquillity as much as they do. After my experience with Mr Fahrenheit, I know that the killer aspect of unwelcome sound is not the decibels but the disempowering feeling of having no control over your own environment and life. Anyone could cope with loud music if they knew that it would soon stop, or could be made to if it didn't.

When I reach my son, I say, 'You can stay here if you want, but I need to go and make a start on lunch.'

'He'll be okay here with me,' says the other boy quickly, alarmed by the prospect of losing his playmate. 'I'm staying out for a bit yet.' He has a Welsh accent, copper-coloured hair and large freckles and, I notice, is dressed like a gentleman farmer – the miniature version – whereas Joseph looks like a city boy in trendy jeans and without a proper coat on, his high-top trainers sitting on the grass next to the trampoline beside a far more appropriate pair of small brown walking boots. I'll have to take him into Spilling and buy him a green padded coat like the Welsh boy's, wellington boots, a cagoule.

'I'm not hungry,' he says. 'I don't want lunch.'

'Okay, stay here, then,' I tell him. 'Come when you're ready. I'll save some pasta for you – you can have it whenever you want.'

Joseph rewards me with a radiant smile. 'Thanks, Mum! You're sick!' This is another word he has picked up at Saviour. He assures me that it means cool and generally brilliant.

I head back to the house, having said nothing to the Welsh boy's mother about keeping an eye on my son. I know I don't need to. The Swallowfield security detail is meticulous. Bethan made it sound too good to be true when I came for the sales tour, but it turns out she was spot on: discreet but ever-present was what she told me and it's quite true. I haven't noticed security staff patrolling the grounds – haven't felt overlooked or spied on at all – but when I left my car window open by mistake, a friendly man in a Swallowfield-crested tunic-top knocked on my door to advise me of my lapse, and when I dropped my phone's case while out for a two-hour walk around the estate that took in Reach Lagoon, Swallows Lake and The Pinnacle, another smiling man in an identical tunic returned it to The Boundary within half an hour of my return.

I love it here. I love everything about it, but especially the benefits I didn't know that I or my family would get when I signed on the dotted line. I knew Swallowfield was beautiful, special, peaceful, but I didn't anticipate the effect it would have on my mental and physical health, or Stuart's, or Joseph's. A mere four days here have extracted the grey-yellow pallor of the city from our skin, the etiolated aspect we didn't know was there until we saw how different we looked after a couple of days breathing in the pure air at Swallowfield. I am not imagining this; Stuart was the one who first remarked on it, and he's right: our skin looks buffed here, rosy pink, properly oxygenated. Our eyes have more shine to them. We are bundles of energy who take far longer to get tired than we did in Cambridge, and when we eventually do it's because we've swum for an hour and a half in the heated outdoor pool and then walked a full circuit of the wild-flower meadow, not simply because we've had to wait twenty minutes in the queue at Tesco on Hills Road and then kick through too many Domino's Pizza boxes on our way back home.

We sleep better here, thanks to the darkness and the silence. The swollen patches beneath my eyes have subsided – this after no cream my Cambridge doctor had me try did any good at all. The same doctor told me I must take at least six months off work and suggested I see a cognitive behavioural therapist. Before we moved into The Boundary, I hadn't been into the office at all for more than a month; I couldn't imagine ever being able to drag myself in there again. Now I am thinking that on 9 January 2013, Joseph's first day back at school, I will be able to report for duty bright and early and tell everyone that I'm fine now, thanks: the trauma is over.

Mr Fahrenheit can try to wind me up by playing choral music if he wants to, but I shall outwit him. I've already told Stuart: we're going to get the attic properly insulated and swap our bedroom with his study. Mr Fahrenheit will have no way of knowing we've done this; he'll never know that there's no longer anyone sleeping in the room on the other side of the wall from his bedroom, and he'll waste hours of his time fiddling with the volume, turning boys' voices up and down in the night whenever Stuart's not there and he thinks he can get away with it. Meanwhile, I will be in the attic, fast asleep, wearing the best earplugs money can buy.

I could and should have thought of this in October or November, but I was in no fit state to save myself then. Swallowfield has saved me, as I knew it would. It's strange. All the things that were out of control and threatening in Cambridge seem manageable from this safe distance. I am ready to throw away the drugs I stole from Mr Fahrenheit's house; I've decided that I will leave the house late one night, while Stuart and Joseph are asleep, and scatter the tiny clumps of cannabis over Topping Lake as if they are the ashes of someone I loved who died. If I'm between my house and the lake, I'm fairly sure no security guard will spot me, as long as I take no more than a few seconds. I don't think it will contravene the estate's no-litter rule; the drugs look like tiny clippings from some kind of tree in any case, so it's all natural and organic; it isn't as if I'm planning to dump a truck load of empty Coke cans. I don't know much about horticulture, but I think it's unlikely that an enormous marijuana plant will start to grow outside my house as a result.

It's strange to think that I brought the drugs to Swallowfield thinking I might need them. Luckily, the security guys don't have sniffer dogs, but still, it was a crazy risk to take – one I only took because the woman I used to be, the Louise Beeston who packed to come here, was well on her way to crazy and heading for a life as a drug addict.

I realise now that, though I never admitted it to myself, that was my back-up plan all along, from the moment I stole the little plastic bag with its illegal contents from Mr Fahrenheit's house: if I couldn't make his noise stop, I could numb myself with drugs instead, so that I didn't care any more – just as soon as I learned how to do that thing with the burned bottle and the silver foil. I might have ended up needing to ask Mr Fahrenheit for lessons.

The memory of my desperation unnerves me as I walk past the entrance to Starling Copse on my way to Topping Lake. I could so easily have failed to save myself. Thank God I didn't; thank God I paid no attention to Pat Jervis, or Stuart, or Alexis Grant. Alexis took great exception when I told her about our plans to buy a second home, as I'd known she would. She winced and said, 'You don't seriously want to be going endlessly back and forth to the Culver Valley, do you? Why not save yourself the hassle and the money and move to a village outside Cambridge instead? You'd have the best of both worlds, like we do in Orwell.'

I smiled and said something non-committal. If she asked me now, I would have an answer for her: I needed, and need, more than the highlights of two worlds squeezed into one. I need two separate worlds: two physically distinct places. I have to know that my Swallowfield life still exists and is waiting to welcome and shelter me whenever I need it to. If you only have one world, one life, then however brilliant it is most of the time, you have nowhere to run when you need to escape from it for a while.

It still shocks me how quickly Swallowfield rescued my sanity. Four days here was all I needed to get me back on track – four days with the guarantee of many more to come – and I am happy again, able to put things in perspective. I know that term time will be hard, with Joseph away at Saviour, but I will simply think about us all being here together during the holidays and I'll be able to get through the weeks of school. And if Stuart can arrange it so that he can work from home more – and he seems fairly confident that he can – that will be even better. In Cambridge, I thought I might prefer it to be just me and Joseph at Swallowfield. The pressure of the city was slowly killing my bond with my husband; here, I have rediscovered it. When we first unlocked The Boundary's front door and walked in, Stuart beamed at me and said, 'Fuck, this is *amazing*, Lou!

You were *so* right about this place. And this house. Look at that view.' That was when I knew we would be okay, that it was safe for me to love him again.

He's on the terrace behind the house when I get back, kneeling beside the new bike we bought for Joseph yesterday, trying to pump up its wheels. 'This pump's knackered,' he says. 'I'm going to have to drive into Spilling and get a new one. Have I got time before lunch?'

'Easily,' I say. It is already what I would normally call lunchtime, but it will take me at least an hour to prepare the food and I don't intend to rush. As Stuart hauls himself to his feet and starts to mutter about finding his wallet and 'bloody bike shop – sold me a dud', I stare at the ripples on the surface of Topping Lake, at the thirty-odd houses that surround it. Winter sun glints off their roofs, lights up the facades of the glass-fronted ones. Each house is unique and yet they look like a coherent collection. Swallowfield has won several prestigious awards, Bethan told me as we took the sales tour – prizes for aesthetics, for ecological soundness, for just about every aspect of its conception and design.

I can see why people would be queuing up to bestow honours. At night all the Topping houses, lit up from the inside, duplicate themselves on the shimmering surface of the lake and it's like looking at a mixed media work of art: light, water, stunning architecture. No wonder most of the houses here don't bother with curtains or blinds apart from in the bedrooms and bathrooms; the estate has been laid out carefully so that no house is intrusively near to any other, and who would want to deprive themselves of such amazing views?

'Right, I'm off,' says Stuart, leaning out of the French doors. I didn't notice him go inside. He's holding his wallet in his hand. 'Oh, before I forget – Dr Freeman rang.'

A stone lands in my heart. A stone thrown from a very long way away. Far enough to be out of reach, I thought. Apparently not.

'Don't panic.' Stuart smiles at the expression on my face. 'What, you think I'm going to say Joseph's Christmas holidays have been cancelled and he has to go straight back to school?'

You've just said it. Why say it if it's not true?

The stone is growing. Hardening.

'Tell me,' I say.

'It was just a reminder about Friday. I must admit, I'd forgotten, but I'm sure you hadn't.'

'Friday? What's happening on Friday?'

'Oh. Well, it's lucky Dr Freeman rang, isn't it? Since we'd both forgotten.' Stuart is trying to make light of it. I am a lead weight. Waiting. 'There's an extra Choral Evensong – last one of the year.'

'On the twenty-first of December?'

That will mean taking Joseph back to Cambridge twice during the holidays. *No. No. I'm not doing it.*

'It's because the chaplain's retiring. It's kind of like a leaving thing for him. Anyway – in view of the Christmas Eve rehearsal and Christmas Day service, I don't think there's much point in our coming back here in between, is there?'

'Yes, there is,' I say quietly. I want to be emphatic but I can't get my voice to carry. 'I'm not going back to Cambridge twice. Neither is Joseph.'

'Don't be silly, Lou. All right, if you want to come back in between, we can. I suppose it's only an hour and a quarter's drive, isn't it? Some people do that twice a day to get to work and back. We can drive back here on the evening of the twenty-first, then back to Cambridge again on Christmas Eve morning. Okay?'

I nod and say nothing, keen for Stuart to leave so that I can allow myself to cry. I'd have liked to stand firm and say no to this extra Choral Evensong – that I'm sure we have never been told about before, that I suspect Dr Freeman of hastily scheduling with the sole aim of destroying my composure and my plans – but I don't want to be unreasonable. Stuart backed down from his initial suggestion that we stay in Cambridge from 21 December until Christmas Day; as soon as he saw how much I hated the idea, he withdrew his proposal. I need to prove that I'm willing to compromise too.

When he finally gets into the car and drives away, I say to myself, 'Right, it's safe to cry now,' and find that I'm unable to. I go inside, close and lock the glass doors and sit down on the sofa. I will remain calm, I promise myself, and deal with this sudden feeling of doom in a rational way. I am not Louise Beeston of 17 Weldon Road any more; I am Louise Beeston of The Boundary, Topping Lake, Swallowfield Estate. I must act and think differently, just as I have furnished my home here differently.

I look around me at the brand new chairs and sofas: all contemporary, bright colours, all bought in one go from Heal's in London and delivered last Friday. No one who saw this room and my lounge in Cambridge would believe that the two might belong to the same family. The furniture in our Weldon Road house is old and shabby, some of it antique, much of it fairly battered from having been dragged by me and Stuart from house to house over the years.

But I'm at Swallowfield now, I remind myself, which means I must be capable of thinking brand new thoughts. I have been up until this point, and I must force myself to continue, since I was doing so well. I have all the natural light I need, fresh air instead of builders' dust, peace and quiet...

Telling myself all this makes me feel a little calmer.

Nothing has really changed. It's only one extra trip to Cambridge, and won't even involve an overnight stay. It won't make any difference. It's the idea of Dr Freeman being able to reach into our Swallowfield life and pluck us out of it at will that has disturbed me, and I've already thought of a solution to that: I will have a word with him at the beginning of next term and tell him that he's not to contact us when we're at Swallowfield – ever. This is our retreat; he must learn to respect that.

I stand, take a deep breath and make my way

across The Boundary's huge open-plan living space towards the kitchen. I am starting to feel hungry, which means that Joseph is bound to be. He could be back any second, demanding the lunch he was so dismissive about half an hour ago.

The kitchen component of our living area is relatively small, but it doesn't matter because the room itself is so vast. I can watch the action on the lake as I prepare food, and there is always some action to watch, whether it's birds hovering, swans gliding, or simply patterns made by light on the gunmetal-grey skin of the water. I can hardly take my eyes off it for long enough to chop a vegetable.

I open the cutlery drawer to pull out my favourite knife. That's when I hear it.

Boys.

Singing.

> O come, O come, Emmanuel,
> And ransom captive Israel,
> That mourns in lonely exile here
> Until the Son of God appear.
> Rejoice! Rejoice!
> Emmanuel shall come to thee, O Israel.

O come, thou Wisdom from on high,
Who orderest all things mightily;
To us the path of knowledge show,
And teach us in her ways to go.
Rejoice! Rejoice!
Emmanuel shall come to thee, O Israel . . .

No boys in sight. These are the same voices I
heard in Cambridge. This is the same choir. I don't
know how I know this, but I do.

O come, thou Rod of Jesse, free
Thine own from Satan's tyranny;
From depths of hell thy people save,
And give them victory over the grave.
Rejoice! Rejoice!
Emmanuel shall come to thee, O Israel . . .

I shut my eyes. No point looking out of any
window for what I know I won't see.

O come, thou Dayspring, come and cheer
Our spirits by thine advent here;
Disperse the gloomy clouds of night,
And death's dark shadows put to flight.

Rejoice! Rejoice!
Emmanuel shall come to thee, O Israel...

I put the knife back in the drawer and close it. Go back to the sofa. Sit very still, waiting for Stuart to come home.

$\diamond$

Stuart closes the lounge door behind him. Leans against it. 'Right,' he says. 'I took him up a sandwich and a drink, and I've started him on FIFA on the Xbox. We should be safe for a while.'

What he means is that Joseph will be safer in a part of the house that doesn't contain his crazy mother. He's right. I don't remember Stuart making a sandwich, and yet I must have been here when he did it. I can see the bread, butter and cheese still out on the countertop, the smeared knife. I haven't moved since Stuart got home.

I don't feel safe. I did until recently – here; only here at Swallowfield, not in Cambridge – but I can't remember the feeling. And so, although I have an idea about what I need to do in order to recreate it, I don't believe it will work. It is hard to imagine myself being able to tap into any kind of calm, ever again.

'Lou——'

'Before you start on me . . . I know it wasn't real.'

Stuart's eyes dart from left to right. Is he looking for clues? A prompt? He wasn't expecting me to say that. He thought he would have to convince me. Now he sees that he doesn't, he has no idea what to say next.

I tell him what he was about to tell me, because I want it to be out there, explicit: the only possible truth. 'Justin Clay's miles away, in Cambridge. Even assuming he could get past the security and break into Swallowfield, there's no way he'd go to all that effort. He might hate me, but not that much.'

'I doubt he does.' Stuart moves away from the door, perches on the edge of the sofa. 'Hate's too strong a word. Minor irritation's probably more like it, assuming you feature in his thoughts at all. It's over from his point of view. He'll have turned his attention back to making money and getting pissed and stoned. You blasted him with loud music, showed him you were his equal, and he caved. What did he say? "Point taken"?'

'"Point made and taken."'

'There you go, then.'

I nod. 'Pat Jervis was right. Apart from the "Best of the Classics" CD that one time, he's only ever played pop music. In his basement. Never played choral music, never anything through the bedroom wall. He doesn't have any CDs of boys' choirs singing. That was all ...' I break off. 'It *felt* real, so real, but ... it can't have been. I see that it wasn't, now. It was all in my head.'

Stuart looks uncomfortable. He's probably wondering whether and when to agree; not too readily, given that he claimed to be able to hear the boys' voices too. He always made sure to say that it was barely audible, he could only just hear it. I understand why. It was his idea of a compromise: supporting me a little bit, while at the same time being fair to Mr Fahrenheit by insisting that the non-existent choral music couldn't be said to constitute a noise nuisance.

It was the opposite of what I needed. He should have given me a shake and said, 'Louise, there is no music playing. None. You're imagining it.' If he'd done that, I might have pulled myself together sooner.

'You never heard it, did you? The choral music.'

'Not really.'

'Not at all.' It's important that we be precise.

Stuart shakes his head. 'Sorry. I only lied because I . . . well, I believed you. At first – until the stuff about Fahrenheit starting off loud and then turning down the volume at the exact moment you woke up – that's when I started to wonder if it might be some kind of paranoid delusion. Before that, I just assumed you could hear it and I couldn't. You're more sensitive to noise than I am.'

'So because you thought I was right and you were wrong, you pretended to hear what I heard?'

'It was the middle of the night, Lou! Every time you asked me! I didn't want to argue, I just wanted to go back to sleep.'

He thinks I'm angry with him. How can he imagine that this is what I want to discuss: his dishonesty, his level of culpability? I don't care that he let me down again. I don't care if every single word that comes out of his mouth is a lie; that's his problem. My only concern at the moment is for my own sanity. If I'm mad, I can't look after my son, and that's all that matters to me: Joseph is the only thing that counts.

'I've thought about it and it all makes sense,' I

tell Stuart. 'I was fine at Swallowfield, absolutely fine, until you told me Dr Freeman had phoned. That's why I heard the boys' choir again. It's a reaction to stress. It must be — some kind of weird... psychosomatic aural hallucination.'

Stuart is nodding. 'I've thought so for a long time,' he says.

Thanks for being too gutless to mention it.

'I'm glad you can acknowledge it. There's no shame in it, Lou.'

'I'm not ashamed.' *I'm frightened.*

'Stress can do strange things to a person. And, look, now that you're aware it's not real, it'll probably stop happening anyway.'

'No, it won't. Not unless I make some changes.' *I'm scared you won't let me. You have to let me.*

Stuart says, 'You've taken the most important step already — admitting it's an illusion. It can't have any power over you once you've seen through it.'

'Can you stop spouting vague platitudes?' I snap. 'It'll happen for as long as there are things in my life that I can't live with. I need to eliminate those things.'

Stuart frowns. 'I don't get it,' he says. 'Didn't we just agree that Mr Fahrenheit—'

'This isn't about Mr Fahrenheit. It's about Dr Freeman.'

'Dr Freeman? What's he got to do with anything?'

I stare down at the floor, thinking that I shouldn't have to spell it out; it should be obvious. And whatever Stuart thinks or wants, or used to think or want, he should be willing to do whatever it takes to make me feel better again. If I can see that I can't go on like this for much longer, why can't he?

I've never felt more alone in my life.

'Oh, God.' Stuart sighs; it goes on for a long time. I hear no concern for my welfare in the sound he makes. 'Lou, please don't say what I think you're going to say.'

The stinging sensation beneath my eyes has returned: just a prickle at the moment – barely noticeable, threatening worse.

'I want to take Joseph out of Saviour,' I say. 'Out of the school and out of the choir.'

'No. No way.'

'There's a reason why I'm hallucinating choral music, Stuart.'

'You said it yourself – you were stressed about Mr Fahrenheit!'

'Yes, but not only about him. And this music I'm hearing that isn't real – it's not Queen, is it? It's not "Don't Stop Me Now". It's boys. Boys in a choir, singing the kind of thing Joseph might sing at Saviour – *has* sung.'

'That doesn't mean—'

'Yes, it does!' Inside me, a dam bursts; desperation gushes out, filling me to the brim. 'What else could it mean? What do you think made me hear a boys' choir again today, if not your news about Dr Freeman's call, his plan to snatch Joseph away for this extra Choral Evensong? It's completely bloody obvious what it means that I keep hallucinating the voices of boys I can't see, and feel as if I'm being tortured – it means I *hate* not having Joseph at home! I can't bear it! And if I don't get him back, if I don't take him out of that school, I'll lose my mind! That's what it means!'

'Louise, can you please get a grip?' says Stuart. 'Shouting's not going to do anyone any good.'

He's wrong; I feel better for having expressed myself without any element of calculation for once – with no fear of the effect my words might have. 'If you don't want a wife who's a wreck, you'll let me take Joseph out of Saviour,' I say quietly, to prove to Stuart that my tone is irrelevant; however I deliver the message, he won't accept it. 'If you want me to go back to work, and be able to cook meals and pay bills and drive the car ... if you care about me *at all*, you'll agree. Please, Stuart!'

'This isn't fair, Lou. You said Joseph could stay at Saviour. You admitted he was thriving there—'

'I'm not thriving.' I cut him off. 'Joseph needs a mother who can function. If only in the school holidays,' I can't resist adding snidely.

'What about our deal? I only agreed to buy a house here because you promised you'd stop cutting up rough about Saviour if I did.'

'I know. I'm sorry.' *Because, after all, you hate Swallowfield so much, don't you, Stuart? That's why you've said it's heaven on earth at least fifty times since we moved in, and how clever I was to spot the ad in the paper.* 'I thought having a home here would be enough,' I say. 'I hoped. But one phone call from Dr Freeman and I'm hearing things again, feeling as threatened here as I did in Cambridge when Mr Fahrenheit's crap music was shaking my floorboards. I didn't realise when we made our deal that I'm going to fall apart if I don't get my son back.' My throat closes on these last words, choking me. 'It's that simple, Stuart.

223

This isn't a whim I've dreamed up out of nowhere. I've really tried, you know. I've given myself every pep talk and lecture and talking-to that I can, and nothing's worked. Losing my son to Dr Freeman is destroying me. I have to take him back.'

Seeing that Stuart's about to protest, I hold up a hand to silence him. 'I know Saviour's a brilliant opportunity, and I'm truly sorry to have to spoil it for Joseph, but there are other schools – day schools, good ones. There are other choirs. It's Cambridge, for God's sake! He can join Jesus's choir – how bad can that be? Jesus College, Cambridge – it's bound to be amazing.'

'Are you asking me or telling me?' says Stuart. 'It sounds to me as if you've made up your mind. What I think's irrelevant.'

'The only thing that's relevant at this point is whether you want a wife who's a gibbering lunatic,' I say, numbed by his lack of empathy. 'Whether Joseph wants a mother who's on suicide watch.'

'Oh, don't be melodramatic! There are other ways that you can ... get better that don't involve ruining our son's potentially amazing musical career – therapy, antidepressants, talking things through with me.'

I want to laugh hysterically. I manage not to.

'How about just giving it a bit more time and seeing if you feel any happier by, say, Easter, or next summer?' Stuart suggests. 'Joseph's only been at Saviour for *one term*! That's no time at all.'

I hear a noise from the hall: the sound of something shifting. Stuart and I look at each other. He heard it too; either that or he's pretending because lying is easier. 'Joseph?' I say. 'Are you there?'

The door clicks open. My beautiful son walks in. He's been crying. I hope Stuart feels as guilty as I do. 'Dad, I don't care about Saviour,' he says in a shaky voice. 'I'll go to any school. It'll be fine. I just don't want Mum to be upset any more.'

Stuart turns on me. 'Well done,' he says angrily. 'I told you to keep your voice down.'

And I don't care what you say, or think, or do. And, apparently, neither does your son.

I open my arms to Joseph. He runs towards me.

8

For the first time since we moved to Swallowfield, I am swimming during the spa's adults-only hours of 7 a.m. to 10 a.m. Apart from me, there is only one other woman here; we have a huge outdoor heated pool all to ourselves, surrounded by wood-and-stone-sculpture-strewn terraces and bordered on all four sides by green hedges as tall as they are thick. Privacy is important to people here. A couple of the homeowners I've spoken to have given the impression that they would ideally like to have Swallowfield's 500 acres all to themselves; they seem rather sensitive about having to share their country estate with others.

I wonder if my fellow swimmer feels that way, and is fuming because I've come along to spoil her solitude. She is evidently a serious sportswoman, with her tight-fitting cap, plastic nose clip and super-fast end-of-length turnaround times, whereas I'm doing a slow length approximately every ten minutes — leisurely breaststroke rather than her turbo-charged front crawl — and quite a lot of aimless drifting in between. I like watching the rabbits pottering about on the grass next to the pool. I love floating on my back and gazing up at clouds and the branches of the tallest trees overhead while my face and the top side of my body chill in the winter air. Plunging fully back into the water afterwards is heaven. When I first arrived, it was raining; I swam a few lengths with the contrast of cold drops splashing on my face and my body immersed in a block of liquid warmth — it was an amazing sensation.

I thought freedom from noise would turn out to be the best thing about Swallowfield, but I was wrong. It's the sheer transcendent beauty of the place; none of its other attributes can compete with that one. Everywhere I turn, everywhere I look, I fall in love with what I see: the fringe of Christmas lights on the spa building's sloped roof, like a trim of glittering silver frost; the spouting fountains at the corners of the pool; the different shades of green beyond; the bare tree and hedge branches reflected in the water; the vast open spaces. My surroundings excite me in a way that they never have anywhere else. Cambridge is full of impressive buildings that I've admired and still admire, but the sight of them has never made my heart hurt with a need to make them part of me. At least four times a day at Swallowfield I think, 'I must never take for granted that I have this in my life.'

I hate to admit it, but it is blissfully, almost hypnotically calm at the spa with no children here. I wouldn't have come for the adults-only session if I'd had my way; I'd have waited until I could bring Joseph with me, but Stuart asked for some time alone with him this morning. It's not a request he's ever made before, and I agreed without question. Maybe he has missed Joseph too, more than he's been willing to acknowledge. Or maybe he wants to explain to our son that he does care about my happiness, whatever impression he might have given yesterday.

Surprisingly, I am not worried that I have been

shunted aside so Stuart can persuade Joseph that it is his destiny to be a Saviour College chorister. I keep asking myself whether this is a real danger that I ought to be concerned about, and concluding that it isn't. Definitely not. Something has changed since yesterday. Stuart was preoccupied and withdrawn last night, then much happier this morning. He was up before me, singing to himself as he loaded the dishwasher. He made a point of coming over to kiss me, and apologised for what he'd put me through. 'I should have paid more attention to how you felt,' he said. 'A lot more.'

'Yes, you should,' I agreed. Keen to capitalise on his good mood, I said, 'I'll make you a deal – if you start now, I'll forgive you for everything.' He nodded as if he understood what I meant, and didn't challenge my implication that there was much to forgive. We couldn't say any more because Joseph came downstairs then, but I am optimistic.

I swim a last length and haul myself out of the water. The shivering dash from the edge of the pool to the door is bearable only because it's so short, and because I can see the sauna and steam room through the glass. I do five minutes in each, with a three-second dip in the indoor plunge pool in between, then head for the ladies' changing room to shower and get dressed. I think again of Stuart loading the dishwasher and decide I want to sing something – people are supposed to sing in showers, aren't they? – but I don't know what. Not anything a choir might sing. Or Queen. In the end I settle on a song I used to love, one that hasn't crossed my mind since I was thirteen: 'Never Surrender' by Corey Hart. Having chosen it, I find I can't sing it; I feel too self-conscious. Who puts this much thought into selecting a shower song? It's not as if I'm a DJ in a fashionable nightclub and my choice really matters. I should have just opened my mouth and let any old thing come out.

I dry my hair, rub some Body Shop Vitamin E moisturiser into my face and make my way back to Topping Lake, thinking that in future I might pay a pound a time and treat myself to a towel from the spa when I swim. I'm always envious of the people I see dropping a white Swallowfield-crested towel into the wooden hamper in the changing room on their way out; it's a pain having to lug a cloth bag full of lumpy wet towel home with me after every swim, and wash it afterwards. And the bag is always still damp the next day, when I want to put a clean, dry towel and swimming costume in it.

I stop in front of The Boundary. There's a car outside it that shouldn't be there, in our visitor parking space. I'm not expecting any guests. Who do I know that drives a blue BMW?

Stuart throws open the front door, beckons me in. I make a questioning gesture with my hands, and mouth the word 'Who?' He mouths something back that I can't decipher, then disappears inside again. I sigh as I walk up our path. Only one way to find out. Whoever it is, Stuart's pleased they're here, so it can't be any of our relatives. Perhaps it's Bethan from the sales office with some goodies left over from someone else's sales tour; she popped round the other day with some chocolates for Joseph that some other children hadn't wanted to eat, silly them. Bethan likes Joseph; whenever I see her she tells me how clever or charming or handsome he is. I find it annoying that she calls him Joe, but it's hard to protest in the face of her barrage of compliments.

With my swimming bag still over my shoulder, I walk into the lounge, eager to see who Stuart is so enthusiastically telling about Swallowfield's keyholder scheme, run by the wonderfully efficient Michelle and Sue who, for a small addition to the standard service charge, are willing to sit in your house whenever you need them to, awaiting delivery of a sofa or a painting if you can't be there to receive it yourself.

At first I don't see who our visitor is; Stuart is standing in the way. When he moves, I see a collage of features and limbs that don't belong in this house, but the one that leaps out at me is the tidy beard like a fitted carpet. Around a smiling mouth.

I gasp and recoil. It's Dr Freeman. Ivan Freeman from Saviour College. Or an apparition that looks exactly like him. Sitting on my sofa, holding a mug from which steam is rising. *No. No. He can't be here. He mustn't be. How could this happen?*

'Hello, Louise,' he says. 'What a fantastic house! And a superb location. I was saying to Stuart, you'd never find Swallowfield unless you were looking and had detailed directions – it's so tucked away.'

Detailed directions. From Stuart. Traitor. Bastard.

'Where's Joseph?' I ask. I picture my son trapped in the boot of Dr Freeman's car, myself screaming as I try to pull it open, but I can't, and Joseph will suffocate if I don't. I've only got a few seconds to save him . . .

'He's upstairs playing on the Xbox,' says Stuart. 'Lou, I promise you, this isn't what it looks like. I didn't invite Dr Freeman here so that the two of us could bully you into accepting a situation you hate. Really.'

Stuart. My first husband.

'Get out,' I say to Dr Freeman. I don't mean to be rude, but they are the only words that suggest themselves. I search my brain for more. 'Joseph's leaving the school and the choir, so there's no reason for you to be here.'

'Lou!'

'I'm sorry if either or both of you are shocked.' I address them as a job lot, feeling no closer to one than the other. 'I'm shocked that you arranged this . . . meeting without consulting me. If I'd been consulted, I'd have refused. I don't want you here, Dr Freeman. Now, please go.'

'I quite understand, Louise. I did say to Stuart that perhaps he ought not to spring this on you.' He is nodding, but not getting up to leave.

'Stuart doesn't care how anything affects me. That's why he didn't take your advice.'

'Lou, that's completely untrue!'

'Louise, listen,' says Dr Freeman. 'I have no wish

to stay here if I'm not welcome, but I think I might have come up with a solution to our problem that we can all be happy with. Please may I put it to you before I go? If you don't like the sound of it, say so and I'll be out of your hair as soon as I can. But ... I've come all this way *not* to collude with Stuart against you, believe it or not, but to offer you terms that I think might make you very happy indeed. It's an offer I've never made to another Saviour family.'

'We're not a Saviour family,' I say. 'We're *my* family. Not yours.'

'Lou, for goodness' sake.' Stuart puts his hand on my arm. I shake him off.

'Fair enough,' says Dr Freeman. 'Point taken. It was a figure of speech, that's all. Let me rephrase — it's an offer no director of music at Saviour has ever made to a choirboy's family. It's unprecedented.'

His words swim in my mind, drifting out of focus when I try to grasp them. *Offer. Unprecedented.*

'Lou?' Stuart prompts. 'Did you hear what Dr Freeman said?'

I heard an introduction, a teaser, that sounded promising, but perhaps that's the ruse: an irresistible lead-in designed to make me believe that something wonderful is coming, so that I mistake whatever comes next for wonderful because I've been groomed. Brainwashed.

I cannot believe that this is anything but a trick.

'There's only one thing you could say that I'd want to hear,' I tell Dr Freeman. 'If Joseph can stay at Saviour and be a chorister and live at home, be a day pupil – great. Anything short of that, no, thank you.'

'What I had in mind is something in between full boarding and day pupil status. I've spoken to the head and our two chaplains, outgoing and incoming.' Dr Freeman pauses to appreciate his own witticism. 'We'd be willing to allow Joseph to spend every Friday and Saturday night at home during term time, as long as you wouldn't mind bringing him in for seven-thirty every Sunday morning. Each week he could spend a significant chunk of the weekend with you, at home – from Friday at four o'clock until Sunday first thing. How does that sound?'

'Lou, it's an amazing offer,' Stuart says. 'I don't see how you can say no. *Two nights a week* at home –'

'And five at school,' I say. Dr Freeman still gets more of my son than I do. Inside me, a huge grey boulder is spiralling a slow descent, rolling over my lungs and gut, squashing them flat. I can't breathe, can't think.

'Louise, I wish I could make you understand how talented Joseph is,' says Dr Freeman. 'I wouldn't be prepared to be flexible in this way for any other boy in the choir at the moment. I can't remember the last time I had as promising a probationer. It would be a devastating blow to lose him.'

'Yes,' I mutter. 'That's how I feel.'

'Lou?' Stuart says hopefully. 'Come on, it has to be a definite yes, doesn't it?' He wants this decided now, nailed down, while Dr Freeman is still in the room.

Fine. Let me nail it down for him. 'No. There are other good schools, other good choirs. If Joseph is as gifted as you say he is, it must be possible for him to have a brilliant musical career without the help of Saviour College.'

Dr Freeman tweaks his grimace into a patient smile. 'Of course. But—'

'I'm sorry, I have to go out now,' I say, cutting him off. If he won't leave, I will.

'Where are you going?' Stuart asks.

'Swimming.'

'But you've just got back from the pool!'

'I've decided I'm going to board at the spa,' I tell him on my way out of the room. I carry on talking to myself as I march out of the house and into the cold. 'Five nights a week. The other two, I'll live at home. As long as you're somewhere else.'

I scratch Dr Freeman's car with my fingernails as I run past it, hurting only myself.

𝄞

I run and run. Across the fields, away from The Boundary, not towards anywhere. I don't mind where I end up, as long as it's far away from Stuart and Dr Freeman. I drop my swimming bag into the brown reeds by the edge of Topping Lake, sick of it weighing me down. *Litter.* Not allowed at Swallowfield, but this isn't an ordinary situation. I wonder if I'll ever find myself in one of those again. It's all I want: normality; not to be scared any more.

I run as fast as I can, as if someone is running after me who will kill me if they catch me. Is Stuart out searching for me? If so, he must have left Joseph alone in the house or with Dr Freeman. Both are unthinkable. I should go back, check my son is all right.

I should go back.

I can't.

A light rain has started; it mingles with the sweat that's pouring down my face. I stop for a second, out of breath, on the stone bridge that leads into Starling Copse. I remember what Bethan told me on our tour: '... the highest density of trees, all evergreens. The homeowners here love having their own private little wood.' That's where I need to go; high density means lots of places to hide, and someone will come looking for me eventually even if they aren't already.

I start running again, along the path that leads to the twelve wooden lodges that were the first to be built here: phase one of Swallowfield, before the architects had the idea of using mainly glass. There would have been no point in Starling Copse; from what I remember of my sales tour, the houses here are circled by tall trees and don't get much natural light anyway.

I feel too visible on the path — anyone could see me — so instead I head across the grass and into the wood. *Keep running, keep running.* I don't want to see anything apart from wood; no way out. Once I'm surrounded on all sides by tree roots and bark and dirt, I feel safer, safe enough to stop for a proper rest. I can hear the rain falling on leaves overhead, but it's not hitting me. Maybe I've reached the centre of the wood, where the overhead cover is thickest. I sink down, intending to sit, but my body gives way and I find myself on all fours like an animal. Everywhere I look, the view is the same: tree trunks, an uneven maze of them, with narrow leaf-strewn dirt paths in between. I try to move my knees and make a squelching sound; I'm stuck in mud, like a car that can't move no matter how hard its wheels spin.

It doesn't matter. I don't want to go anywhere. I feel more protected here than I would in my own house – in either of my houses. I want to burrow in and bury myself, sink down and never come up for air. I fall on to my stomach, lie flat against the ground, with my cheek pressed against the wet mud. It feels oddly satisfying. Swallowfield's spa should consider offering it as an off-site treatment: the Outdoor Mud Experience.

The thought shocks me; it's the kind of thing I might have thought before. Before what, though?

I haul myself up and into a sitting position, wiping the mud from my face with the sleeve of my shirt. What has just happened? Maybe nothing. Maybe something that most people – sane people – would regard as trivial. The physical evidence of my shaking body proves only that I am very upset.

Stuart and Dr Freeman cooked up a deal without telling me. It was a deal I could never accept, but perhaps they didn't realise that. Perhaps they both genuinely thought I'd be delighted by the offer.

Stuart invited Dr Freeman to our house at Swallowfield without consulting me, without warning me. Is it reasonable to expect him to have known that my safe haven would be ruined the second that anybody from Saviour crossed the threshold? Probably not; I have never told him in so many words how important it is to me to keep our Swallowfield life and our Cambridge life completely separate.

I could forgive those two transgressions, but not the third. *Lou? Come on, it has to be a definite yes, doesn't it?* I will always be able to hear him saying those words in my head.

I feel tears starting and see no reason to subject them to any kind of restriction. I cry fiercely, for a long time, to the sound of the rain drumming on my roof of leaves. There couldn't be a more appropriate backing track. If I were sobbing like this in the sky, my tears would make exactly the noise I can hear.

How dare Stuart try to bully me into making up my mind about something so important in the presence of a man he knows I distrust? How can I ever feel love for him again, with the memory of that in my mind?

I don't know how much time passes before I realise that I can't feel anything but painful tingling in my legs. Pins and needles; I've been sitting in this position for too long. I stand up and hobble around until the uncomfortable prickling stops and I can walk easily again. I need to get out of this wood and back to my son now that I'm capable of stringing a few sensible thoughts together, now that I can feel my legs and my anger towards my husband.

I am me again, no longer a wild animal. If Dr Freeman is still at The Boundary, I'll be able to cope better: at least it won't be a surprise like the first time. I will evict him, with the help of Swallowfield's security staff if necessary, and then

I'll give Stuart an ultimatum: either he agrees to take Joseph out of Saviour — completely, with no caveats — or else our marriage is over.

I almost hope he refuses, so that I can experience the adrenalin rush of expelling him from my life. Though if he agrees to everything I want, I will be pleased in a less visceral, more rational way. I'll get my son back in a way that allows him to keep his father too. No doubt my resentment towards Stuart would subside over time, like a painful swelling.

I can see both sides. This more than anything reassures me that I am ready to try and find my way home. I don't know how I'll explain why I'm covered in mud; I'll worry about that later. First things first: I need to get out of this wood. It's strange to think that only fifteen or twenty minutes ago I wanted to immerse myself in it so that I couldn't see the edges. That same desire is still bubbling inside me, deep down, but the voice that says I mustn't act on it is stronger. No one who has a child can afford to lose themselves for ever.

If I don't return to The Boundary, Joseph will have only Stuart to rely on. The prospect horrifies me.

I start to walk between the trees, picking a

direction at random. I'm not going to panic. I have my phone with me, in my pocket. If I were to get seriously lost, I could ring Stuart and...

My phone. I scrabble for it with muddy fingers, pull it out of its case, keen to see if there's a message for me.

My husband has sent me a text. Ten minutes ago. 'I've got rid of Dr Freeman. Safe to come back, assuming you're willing to talk about this like grown-ups? Joseph fine – still playing on Xbox upstairs, blissfully unaware. S.'

In all the time I've known Stuart, he has never signed a text or email with a kiss – not once.

I trudge through mud until I see, in the distance, something that isn't trees: a perfectly square wooden house standing alone on a small grass-covered island, close to the edge of an expanse of water that's too small to be a lake, I think, though I don't know what else to call it. It's long and thin, not much wider than the island that protrudes from it. And the water is moving sideways quite fast; does this mean it's a stream?

The house is unmistakably Swallowfield-architect-designed, and I wonder why I didn't spot it when Bethan drove me around; I thought she'd shown me everything, but there's no way I wouldn't have noticed a wooden cube house with an island all to itself. Automatically, I try to assess its position in the Swallowfield housing hierarchy: the system that no residents ever mention, but we all know is there. The Cube (that must surely be its name, or someone has missed a trick) is smaller than most of the properties here, and the glass houses are seen as preferable to the wooden ones on the estate, but surely hundreds of superiority points would have to be awarded for private island status? Perhaps this is why The Cube isn't included in the sales tour – if there is only one house in this special position and it's already taken, why drive other prospective buyers wild with envy?

As I get closer, I see that there's a raised walkway leading from the edge of the field that borders the water to the little island. I hear something too. Music. From an open window. Good. This must mean someone's in; hopefully they'll be able to direct me back to Topping Lake and won't report me for the heinous crime of trespassing on their land and privacy. Is whoever owns the house also the leasehold owner of the island? That too would make a difference, hierarchy-wise. Before Stuart and I bought The Boundary, we were sent plans with a red line drawn around the exact part of Swallowfield that we would own: the house itself and the twenty or so square metres between it and Topping Lake.

The music starts to sound familiar as I get closer to the house, but the wind carries the notes away before I can identify the song. There are lights on. A woman at the window. Is that ... Bethan?

It is. It's her. She's moving around behind what I guess must be the kitchen window; she looks as if she's putting things away. Either this is a new show home and she's sorting it out, or else she has a house at Swallowfield herself.

I hurry towards her, waving to catch her attention, then stop when I hear a tune that knocks the breath out of me, and lyrics that seem to be all about my Cambridge next-door neighbour.

Mr Fahrenheit.

'Don't Stop Me Now' by Queen.

No. Not here. It can't be.

But why not? If he was ingenious enough to find a way to play music on the street so that no one but me would hear it, he can do anything.

I stand, still and solid, unable to move, subject

to a law that's the opposite of gravity: shocked bolt upright. Bethan will deny everything, of course.

'Louise? Is that you?' She pushes the window open wider and leans out. 'Hang on, let me turn the radio down.' She ducks back into the house. Mr Fahrenheit's musical manifesto subsides.

When she reappears, I say, 'How much is he paying you?'

'Sorry?'

'How much is Justin Clay paying you?'

'Who? Sorry, you've lost me!' Bethan smiles. He must have chosen her for her innocent face. If she genuinely doesn't understand what I mean, why doesn't she look puzzled instead of so blandly friendly and well-intentioned? Why isn't she asking me more questions?

'Why didn't you tell me you've got a house here?' I ask.

She looks uncomfortable. 'Do you want to come in for a coffee, so we can have a chat?'

'No. I want to know what you and Justin Clay are planning. I assume it involves driving me mad at Swallowfield, like he did in Cambridge? How do you know him? How long? Whatever he's told you about me, it's not true. I don't deserve this.'

'Louise, I don't know who you're talking about.'

'Whatever he's paying you, I'll pay you more!' I shout.

'You seem very upset. Why don't you—'

'Why don't *you* fuck off?' I yell at her, because I can't bear to listen to any more lies. I turn and run back the way I came, back into the trees and the darkness.

&

I hear their voices as I enter the woods again. I know who they are without knowing their names. Their names don't matter; I will know them when I need to. I'm not worried about being lost, though the trees have formed a ring around me and seem not to want to let me pass. I know the voices will lead me home.

That's where I will find them: at The Boundary.

I walk slowly. There is no need to run; if I ran, I might scare them away. I must arrive at the house at the right moment — not too soon. The song has only just started. I can hear it faintly, in the distance, drawing me like a magnet. I follow the melody.

O come, O come, Emmanuel,
And ransom captive Israel . . .

One foot, another foot. One note, another note. Boys' voices marching me home, telling me which way to go. Bethan and Mr Fahrenheit: it doesn't matter any more, whatever they're doing. The choir is all that matters: they're the ones I must listen to, the only ones.

. . . That mourns in lonely exile here
Until the Son of God appear.
Rejoice! Rejoice!
Emmanuel shall come to thee, O Israel . . .

They get louder as I get nearer. I'm back at the entrance to Starling Copse. Inconceivable, now, to think that Dr Freeman was at Swallowfield today. He was here in the way that Stuart is here: not seeing, not understanding – presence that's a kind of absence. They weren't in the same place as me or the choir.

I don't understand it yet, but I will. The boys' voices sing me a promise that I will soon make sense of everything. All I need to do is keep listening.

... O come, thou Wisdom from on high,
Who orderest all things mightily ...

I pass the trampoline and the tennis court. Swallowfield is still in every detail, silent apart from the choir. The clouds above are fixed in place, not drifting. There's no shaking of leaves, no breeze to disturb the grass. No breath but mine, and mine makes no movement in my chest. I could be travelling through a landscape architect's three-dimensional model laid out on a 500-acre table. I could be a plastic figure on a board that someone has taken out of a box and unfolded − at the moment. I will become real when I am shown the truth.

... To us the path of knowledge show,
And teach us in her ways to go.
Rejoice! Rejoice!
Emmanuel shall come to thee, O Israel ...

I am coming. I have to get home before the song ends, but I don't know how much of it is left. As I approach Topping Lake, I feel myself being pulled faster. It's like suction. I'm not even sure if

I'm walking any more. I am drifting, gliding, as the motionless clouds stare down at me. They are all in on the secret: the clouds, the hedges, the fields, the jetties, the wooden bird hides. The landscape knows. Swallowfield knows.

> . . . *O come, thou Rod of Jesse, free*
> *Thine own from Satan's tyranny;*
> *From depths of hell thy people save,*
> *And give them victory over the grave.*
> *Rejoice! Rejoice!*
> *Emmanuel shall come to thee, O Israel . . .*

There's a space where Dr Freeman's car was. Good. I don't need to think about him any more. I must make room in my mind for what I'm about to learn. All other thoughts fall to the ground: leaves in autumn. Natural. It's nothing to be scared of as long as I don't look away. As long as I let myself see.

> . . . *O come, thou Dayspring, come and cheer*
> *Our spirits by thine advent here;*
> *Disperse the gloomy clouds of night . . .*

The Boundary's front door is open. Stuart is standing in the way. I feel sorry for him because he has to say so much that I won't hear. He has started already. Without guidance, there is no way for him to know there's no point, and I can't tell him. I can't explain because I am too busy listening: the guided, not the guide, not yet. I push past him, walk to the foot of the stairs. Stop. The voices are really loud here.

. . . And death's dark shadows put to flight.
Rejoice! Rejoice!
Emmanuel shall come to thee, O Israel . . .

Upstairs: that's where I have to go. To the master bedroom. My bedroom. That's where it is. Slowly, I ascend. 'Don't follow me,' I say. I am the follower. Chosen. He is the left behind. I can't take him with me for this. 'Look after Joseph. Keep him downstairs.'

I pull open the bedroom door and, in the same moment, hear it slam shut. What was in front of me is now behind; I am in the room, unaware of having moved forward from the landing, no memory of crossing over.

I fumble for the light switch. Press it. Nothing happens. The room is still dark. It was light when I arrived at the house – midday – but in this room it's as dark as if someone had taped over the glass to exclude all natural light.

That happened once before, in a house that was also mine.

Except they can't have done that here. If they had, the view would have disappeared along with the light, and it hasn't. I can see everything. At last.

The double doors to the balcony that overlooks the lake are wide open.

They're there: the choir. I try to count them, but they shift and reassemble. Sometimes there are hundreds of them, sometimes only sixteen, like in Joseph's choir, but I can see each of their faces so clearly. They must be at least 100 metres from where I'm standing, but their noses and mouths and eyelashes brush against my skin as they sing.

I shouldn't need to ask who they are. I will see them again and I will know. I can't ask because their singing is too loud. Almost deafening.

. . . O come, thou Key of David, come,
And open wide our heavenly home;

Make safe the way that leads on high,
And close the path to misery.
Rejoice! Rejoice!
Emmanuel shall come to thee, O Israel . . .

There are girls as well as boys. Yes, of course. I
think I know who they are now. But I would still
like to ask.

Eight boys or hundreds of boys. Eight girls or
hundreds of girls. Out above the water, floating
over the centre of Topping Lake, where the moon
was last night.

Like the moon, they glow silver: the colour of
the Swallowfield Christmas lights – a jagged moon
made up of the shapes of children, the girls' long
hair streaming in the air, eyes glittering, faces pale
and bright. They look so cold: child sculptures
carved out of ice, except they're scream-singing as
if they're afraid no one will hear them.

As if they're afraid I don't hear them.

Their eyes lock on to mine, stick into me like
pins, their irises blueish-white. I open my mouth to
try to tell them that I'm here and they don't need
to sing so loud – they're not allowed to; they will
be stopped if they continue to make such a noise;

someone will complain – but I can't find the words I want, only the words of their song. I am singing with them.

> *. . . O come, O come, great Lord of might,*
> *Who to thy tribes on Sinai's height*
> *In ancient times once gave the law*
> *In cloud and majesty and awe.*
> *Rejoice! Rejoice!*
> *Emmanuel shall come to thee, O Israel . . .*

Stuart is banging on the door, asking what I'm doing, what's wrong with me. Demanding that I come out. I can't. I don't know why he doesn't come in. Perhaps for the same reason. I have an open door in front of me: I can leave him behind, get closer to the choir. I know that's what they'd like me to do.

I step out on to the balcony. The damp wood chills the soles of my feet. When did I take my shoes and socks off? I don't remember doing it. The children in the choir have bare feet too, dangling: like white upside-down hands, waving from beneath their robes.

I climb down the wrought-iron spiral staircase to the terrace below. Round and down, like a stone.

As I run to the lake, I am pushed back. Something wants to stop me from moving forward. The children start to fade. 'No!' I cry out. 'Where are you going?'

I hear Stuart scream my name. The sound of the choir is still audible, but receding, as if it's coming from further away.

> ... *O come, thou Root of Jesse's tree,*
> *An ensign of thy people be* ...

'Come back!' I call.

I drag my body forward, to the edge of the water. Should I go down the mud steps? They were cut into the grass verge for easy access to the lake in summer, Bethan told me. If I take one step towards the water, will the choir reappear? Is that where they are — under the surface?

'Louise? Where are you? Are you out here?'

Stuart. He's on the terrace. No, he mustn't leave Joseph alone inside. We have to work together to keep our son safe.

I'm scared of Stuart. Joseph should be too. He will try to stop us.

I sink down to my haunches. It's impossible to

see anything by the lake in darkness like this, but I'm scared Stuart will find me. That's why the choir disappeared: they knew he was coming.

'Lou?' he calls again. Nearer this time.

I want to run, but I'm blinded by the blackness that the children left when they took their jagged choir moon away and left an empty sky. I take a step to the left, then another to my right, but each time I draw back, thinking I can hear Stuart's breathing.

Suddenly, everything is moving, whispering: the trees, the bushes, the tarpaulins stretched over the garden furniture on the terrace of every house around Topping Lake. It's not just Stuart coming for me, it's one man from each house. They are all him. They are coming from all sides.

I can't stay out here any more. I need to see light so that I know my eyes are still working, that I haven't gone blind. How did I let myself get so far from my house? Stupid. Crazy. I feel as though I'm miles from home, further than I've ever been.

I must sing. If I sing it might bring them back.

. . . Before thee rulers silent fall;
All peoples on thy mercy call.

Rejoice! Rejoice!
Emmanuel shall come to thee, O Israel . . .

Faintly but unmistakably, I hear the children singing with me. Time-lagged, like an echo. I crawl along the edge of the lake on my hands and knees, looking for their reflection in the water, but I see nothing until I close my eyes, panting in panic, and find colours on the insides of my eyelids. Purples, reds. It comforts me and gives me the answer. That's it, I think. I need to get back to safety, back to the lights and colours of my house. To The Boundary.

I stand up and turn round. Open my mouth to scream and choke on the loud singing that pours out of their mouths and into mine, millimetres from my face as my eyes hit the glass.

There they are. There they always were.

Blazing with light, hair streaming. In my house, behind the windowpane, hanging there, suspended from nothing; nothing in the room but them and the blinding glare. They're so close, I can see the pupils of their eyes widen and shrink. Watching them draws all the breath from my lungs, and more of the song from my mouth. We are singing all together now.

. . . O come, Desire of nations, bind
In one the hearts of all mankind;
Bid thou our sad divisions cease,
And be thyself our King of Peace.
Rejoice! Rejoice!
Emmanuel shall come to thee, O Israel . . .

'Who are you?' I ask through the words of the hymn. It's a code. Only the choir could hear the true meaning under the cover of the words I am singing. Stuart wouldn't understand, and besides, I've left him outside. He won't be able to get back in, not while the choir is in the house.

A boy in the front row with hair as long as some of the girls' says, 'We're the Orphan Choir.'

Yes. That's who you are.

'What are your names?'

A few of them answer. *Alfie Speake. George Fairclough. Lucinda Price.*

I know those names. All of them. 'Thank you for coming,' I say. We hide all of this beneath the hymn.

. . . O come, O come, Emmanuel,
And ransom captive Israel,

That mourns in lonely exile here
Until the Son of God appear.
Rejoice! Rejoice!
Emmanuel shall come to thee, O Israel.

I know them, and I sing with all their voices. I sing, 'The Orphan Choir, the Orphan Choir, the Orphan Choir.'

9

'Were you going to throw yourself in?' Stuart asks.

'No. I don't think so. I don't know.' Only one day later, but it feels like a year. 'It's hard to remember. I . . . wasn't in control.'

'At one point you started to walk down the steps into the water. You must remember what was going through your mind when you did that.'

'I don't. I really don't, Stuart.'

'Why did you push the bedside cabinet in front of the bedroom door? What did you plan to do in there that you didn't want me to see? If you wanted to throw yourself in the lake, why go up to the bedroom first, and down the spiral staircase? Why come into the house at all?'

Telling him why would involve trying to explain that the 'why' didn't belong to me. That would lead us to questions of how. *I don't know. I agree: there's no way. All I know is that it happened.*

'I don't have any of the answers you want,' I say. 'I'm sorry. I wasn't . . . That wasn't me.'

'But you are now,' he accuses.

'Yes.'

'How is that possible?'

He is interrogating me the way a policeman would. I'm glad of his strictness. I need his ruthless logic to scare the inexplicable away.

I also need to tell him that it was real and I know what it meant, but if I do, he will write me off as certifiable. He'll say it's impossible, completely irrational.

So we have a problem: a paradox. I want him to negate what happened with his disbelief, and yet I need him to believe me so that he can help me to save us. That I can put the dilemma to myself in these terms convinces me, if no one else, that I am not crazy.

I will sound crazy if I tell Stuart what happened.

Better to let him think I took off my shoes and socks and sang a hymn by the lake for a reason neither of us knows.

'You need to apologise to Bethan,' he says, resting his head in his hands as if his neck can't bear its weight any more. He's sitting on the floor of our bedroom, leaning against the closed balcony doors. I'm on the edge of the bed, my bare feet touching the floor, like a hospital patient who hasn't walked unaided for a long time. Joseph is at the Welsh boy's house: a temporary evacuee, sharing a normal morning with a normal family, or so Stuart hopes. 'Sooner rather than later, ideally,' he says, but I've lost the thread and can't pin down what he means. 'I can't believe you swore at her, Lou. Poor old harmless Bethan!'

Right. Bethan.

'I know,' I say. 'I'll go round and see her. She'll understand.'

Stuart laughs bitterly. 'If she does, can you ask her if she'd mind explaining it to me?'

'I'll tell her the truth – I've no idea what came over me. Only that . . . it was something bad.' Our shared experience was worse for me than it was for Bethan. Can I risk telling her that without causing offence? Probably not. 'I'm not even . . .' I break off.

'What?'

'I couldn't swear that her radio was playing "Don't Stop Me Now". Maybe it was a different song playing, not the one I heard. Maybe she didn't have a radio on at all! Look, I don't know, okay? Don't recoil! None of this is my fault! When things happen that you think can't happen, you start to wonder about everything. I'll go and grovel to Bethan and sort it out. I'll take her a bottle of wine.'

'Don't. Any wine we've got, I'm going to need.'

I look at him to see if he's joking. He isn't.

'Stuart?'

'Mm?'

'Do you believe in premonitions?'

'No.'

'I mean . . . not seeing exactly what's going to happen in the future or anything like that, but . . . some kind of warning?'

'No,' he says flatly. 'I believe you're cracking up. That's what I believe. We need to get you back to Cambridge, soon as possible, and—'

'No!' The threat of a premature return to our Cambridge life helps me to focus. 'Stuart, do you want me not to be mad any more? Do you want things to be like they were before? Before Joseph started at Saviour?'

'Yes. If they can be.' His voice is full of fear: fear of the wrong thing.

'They can,' I say with certainty. 'But . . . how much do you want them to? Would you give *anything*?'

Silence for a few seconds.

'Yes.'

'Then listen to me now, do what I say, and I promise you – I swear on all our lives – things will go back to normal.'

'Lou, you're not well enough to—'

'Listen.' I speak over him. 'We need to take Joseph out of that school and out of the choir. If we do that, everything will be fine. If we don't, we'll die.'

Stuart starts to cry. 'My God, Lou. Listen to yourself.'

'I'm sorry. I know it isn't pleasant to hear, but it's the truth.'

'We'll *die*? What, all three of us?'

I expected him to ask me how I know, what happened to make me believe this. I'm glad he hasn't; I wouldn't have told him. The less I say, the better. There's only one detail that matters anyway:

the danger we must do everything to avoid. Heeding the warning.

'No, not Joseph,' I say. 'Joseph will live, and Alfie Speake will live, and George Fairclough and Lucinda Price, and whatever her brother's called, but you and I will die. So will other choir parents. Perhaps all of them.' I can't work out if it's all or only most. I didn't see Nathan Grant, Alexis's son, in the Orphan Choir. I don't think I saw Donna McSorley's son Louis either.

Stuart stands up, wipes his tears away with his hands. 'I won't listen to this rubbish,' he says. 'You don't know what you're saying.'

'Yes, I do. I know exactly what I'm saying. Agree to Joseph leaving Saviour or else I'll leave you today and take him with me, and never come back. Agree to him leaving and I'll do whatever you want — see a shrink for the rest of my life if you think I need to.' I have a better idea: more selfless. Nobler. 'Or you keep Joseph, lock me away in a secure unit for nutters and find yourself a new wife — anything, as long as you agree to take him out of that school.' I would give up everything, even my son, to save him from becoming an orphan.

'Jesus, Lou. How can you—'

SOPHIE HANNAH

'Say yes and I *promise* you, Stuart, everything will be fine.' I have to make him agree. 'Look, what if we just try it? You heard what Dr Freeman said about Joseph, how brilliantly talented he is – he'd have him back like a shot, any time. If I'm wrong, if we take him out of Saviour and I'm still mad two weeks later, I'll never ask for anything again, but ... *please*, just do what I ask, just this once.'

Silence stretches across the room between us. 'You're right,' Stuart says eventually. 'Dr Freeman would take Joseph back. Even if he left.'

'Then you agree?' I need to hear him say it. I can't allow myself to hope until I have.

'Not because I share your ridiculous paranoia that's based on nothing.'

It wasn't nothing. Yesterday's visitation wasn't nothing.

'I'll go along with your plan because I'm desperate,' Stuart says.

As desperate as I am. Finally. Thank God.

'That's the only reason. I want you back – the old you. If there's even a tiny chance ...' He shakes his head sadly.

'Wait and see,' I tell him. 'You won't regret it. You'll get the old me back.'

'I'm not sure I will – not so easily. I don't want to

lie to you, Lou. Or mislead you, even. You need to know that I think you're in pretty serious trouble. Mentally. All right, Joseph boarding might have sparked it off, but I can't believe it doesn't go quite a bit deeper.'

'Wait and see, Stuart. I promise you — let me take Joseph out of Saviour and I'll be fine. We'll all be fine.'

'All right, then, here's the deal,' he says. 'When does next term begin?'

How can he not know the date? Saviour's calendar is pinned up on the kitchen noticeboard at Weldon Road; it's burned into my brain: the day Dr Freeman will reclaim my son if I don't stop him.

'January the ninth,' I say, scared again. Why is Stuart trying to offer me a deal when he's only just agreed to mine? I don't want to talk about this any more. I have things to do, important things. I have to apologise to Bethan, then ring round other Cambridge schools and choirs to see which have places for Joseph.

'If you still feel the same way on January the eighth, I won't argue with you,' Stuart says. 'We'll take Joseph out of Saviour, no questions asked. But in the meantime ... we go to this extra Choral

Evensong as planned. He does the Christmas Day service.'

'No! He leaves now – we email Dr Freeman today.'

'Lou, that's not fair. We're surely not going to die between now and Christmas Day?' Stuart attempts a laugh. It comes out as a bark.

But he's right: the danger is in February, not between now and Christmas. The first danger, anyway. Unless I'm wrong.

I don't think I am.

Can I risk it? *No. I don't want to.*

Stuart sits down on the bed beside me and takes my hand in both of his. Feeling the warmth of his skin, I am suddenly aware of how cold I am. 'Lou,' he says. 'Our son was picked from hundreds of boys to be a member of Saviour College choir. That was and is an amazing achievement.'

'I know.'

'I'd like him to do one Christmas service as a Saviour chorister. Please. I tell you what – on Boxing Day, if you haven't changed your mind, I'll ring Dr Freeman and tell him Joseph's leaving. First thing Boxing Day.'

No. Absolutely not.

'You have my solemn promise. But...please let him do these last two services. Let's hear him sing with his choir a couple more times. I've been looking forward to it.'

I nod. 'Okay. If it's so important to you.' *No, no, no. On no account.*

Between now and Friday, I must find a way to stop this from happening and still get what I want. I'll think of something; I have to. I can't let Joseph do Choral Evensong. Or the service on Christmas morning. I can't let him anywhere near Saviour's choir ever again.

'Thank you, Lou.'

As Stuart kisses my forehead, I wonder if I could make him too ill to travel on Friday without doing him any serious harm. I would never dream of doing that to Joseph, but to Stuart...maybe.

♪

Bethan's square wooden house turns out not to be called The Cube but The Hush. 'I thought of the name myself,' she says proudly as she puts the kettle on to make us both a coffee. Her kitchen/dining/living area is open-plan, like The Boundary's, and

colour-coordinated to within an inch of its life —
depressingly so. The cushions are the same yellow
as the kettle and the mugs; the coasters, throws and
rugs all contain yellow, beige and green, which are
also the colours of the bland abstract prints on the
walls.

'Normally new homeowners pick a house name
from the estate's list, but you can choose your own
if you want, as long as the board approves it. The
Hush went through with no hassle — they only really
object if someone wants to use something that's
not in keeping with the ethos and atmosphere of
Swallowfield. Once we had a chap who applied for
permission to use the name This Is My Smallest
House.' Bethan giggles. 'He meant it in a tongue-
in-cheek way, but the board thought some people
might take offence. It was one of the biggest houses
he was buying, and other homeowners might have
thought he was boasting.'

I wonder if I should interrupt her flow, try again
to apologise. I tried as soon as she opened the door,
several times, but she wouldn't let me. 'Let's put it
behind us and move on,' she insisted, beaming at
me. 'I could tell you weren't yourself yesterday.'

I'm grateful for her willingness to let bygones be

bygones, but also suspicious of it. Why won't she let me explain even a little bit? Has she really cast it from her mind as if it never happened? How can she have? If someone I knew who had previously always been friendly and polite suddenly swore at me for no reason, I'm pretty sure I'd want to hear what they had to say about it afterwards.

Perhaps Bethan's cheery banter is a cover for embarrassment: she doesn't want to get into a heavy or awkward conversation. Which would be fair enough. She hardly knows me, really.

'The Hush is the perfect name for this house,' she says. 'It's *so* quiet. I mean, the whole of Swallowfield's quiet, obviously, but here you literally don't even hear another voice from one day to the next. That's why I sometimes have the radio up quite loud – there's no danger of anyone being disturbed by it. Apart from you, no one's ever wandered over here before. I don't know how you managed to find it – it's really tucked away, on the far side of Starling Copse. Most of our homeowners don't know this little area exists. To be honest, the board kind of made that a condition when I told them I wanted to buy.'

She brings our coffees over to the lounge part

of the room, hands me mine. I expect her to sit opposite me in one of the two armchairs, but instead she sits beside me on the sofa. A strange choice; now I will have to move either my head or my body in order to see her. She's wearing too much perfume. It smells the way fruit with far too much sugar on it would taste. I wonder if she's one of those women who gets all drunk and giggly on nights out and then expects other women to share a toilet cubicle with her as a sign of close friendship.

'When I first started here as sales director, I never for one minute imagined I'd end up buying a house,' she says. 'I couldn't afford it, to be honest, not even one of the apartments over by the main playground, but then I fell head-over-heels in love with the place. I had to buy a house here, I *yearned* to. So we did.' She smiles, but not happily. There's a sadness in her voice too. 'We sold our house in Rawndesley — downsized to a two-bedroom flat. It's a bit poky, but I've never regretted it.'

Then why do you sound as if you do?

'Swallowfield had to come first.' Bethan nods as if to assure herself that she's right. 'If you've got two homes, it makes sense to have the best one in your favourite place, like my husband said at the

time. And how could Swallowfield not be anybody's
favourite place? It's like paradise, isn't it?'

It wasn't like paradise yesterday. I'm starting to feel
as if I might have to leave in a hurry. Normally I
can handle small talk as well as the next person, but
today it feels almost negligent to be indulging in it.
I'm not sure I can fight the rising tide of everything
I'm not saying for much longer.

'Trouble is, it's obviously a bit funny for one
of the Swallowfield sales team to be a homeowner
too – bit of a conflict of interests, maybe?' Bethan
prattles on. 'That was the board's worry. They didn't
want to lose me as sales director, though – not to
blow my own trumpet, but I'm pretty good at my
job – so they offered to build me a house miles away
from any other homeowners, at a knock-down price,
and here we are! The Hush.' She looks admiringly
around her own lounge. 'I was amazingly lucky. But,
much as I'd love to rave about my lovely home at
Swallowfield when I'm showing prospective buyers
round, the board asked me not to. That's why I didn't
say anything to you about living here. I think they
think ... well, I've got my own island, haven't I? I
can hardly say, "Sorry, none of the other properties
have got that, only mine." The sort of people who

come here wouldn't take kindly to a sales pitch from someone with a better second home than she's offering them. Not that the other houses aren't just as special in their own way,' Bethan adds quickly as she realises what she's said and how I might take it. She pats my arm. 'Yours is particularly lovely – I've always thought that.'

'The music you were playing yesterday, when I was outside,' I blurt out. 'What was it?'

'Music? Oh, you mean on the radio? I don't remember. Why?'

'Was it "Don't Stop Me Now" by Queen? If it wasn't, then I really am losing my mind.' I start to weep, except it doesn't feel as if it's coming from me. It's as if a flood has started inside me without warning. Normally I know a few seconds in advance when I'm about to start crying; I can get away from whoever I'm with and do it in private. I hate crying in front of people.

I try to apologise but can't get the words out through the tears.

Bethan takes the mug from my hands and puts it down on the coffee table next to her. I pray that she won't hug me or, even worse, pat me on the back. If she says and does nothing, and doesn't touch me, I might be able to pull myself together. 'I think it was,' she says. 'It was definitely something by Queen. Yes, I'm pretty sure it was "Don't Stop Me Now".'

I pull my bunched fists out of my eyes and look up at her. She's frowning. Wanting to be certain she's given me the right answer. I feel guilty for thinking bad thoughts about her perfume, and her bathroom habits.

'Louise, what's wrong?' she says gently. 'I don't want to pry, and you don't have to talk about it if you don't want to but ... well, I'm always happy to listen. And I never judge.'

How is that possible? I judge all the time. So does everybody I know: Stuart, my family, his family, my colleagues, the choir parents, Dr Freeman, Mr Fahrenheit. Even Pat Jervis, who has no bloody right.

I wonder if 'I never judge' is the polite way of saying, 'So you'd better not judge me.' If so, I can't imagine that it's a particularly effective strategy. The judgemental would surely blacklist the non-judgemental ahead of any other group.

I can't figure Bethan out. At all.

The urge to cry is gone, completely vanished.

SOPHIE HANNAH

I couldn't if I wanted to, even though my face is still wet. What I feel compelled to do instead is tell the story from the beginning. To someone who isn't Stuart, someone who doesn't know me very well and is capable of being objective because there's nothing at stake for her. Someone whose reaction I can't predict: a woman who sits too close to me on the sofa but doesn't hug me when I burst into tears. Who appreciates the beauty of Swallowfield, but furnishes and decorates her home here like a buy-to-let inner-city landlord with no time and little imagination.

I want to know what Bethan thinks. I need to know.

I tell her everything – the whole story, even the parts of it that I might have imagined or hallucinated. I tell her about Mr Fahrenheit, Pat Jervis, Joseph being a boarder at school and how much I hate it, the choral music that I heard in my bedroom and then on the street – the music no one else heard.

And then, because I can't allow the secret to swell inside me any longer, I tell her about the Orphan Choir. She listens without interrupting, without looking scornful. When I get to the end of the story and she's sure I've finished, she hands me my mug of coffee. 'It'll be cold by now, but...' She shrugs.

'Thank you.' I take a sip. It tastes disgusting.

'I can make you another one if you like? A hot one.'

Then why wait to offer until I'm drinking the cold one again?

'This is fine,' I say.

'My son's very musical too,' Bethan says. 'Ed, he's called. He's nine, so a bit older than Joseph, but he's in his school choir. He's one of the best singers they've got, and I'm not just saying that because I'm his mum. It's only a state school – we can't afford private – but the music teacher's brilliant. They learn all sorts – songs in Latin, Irish folk music. They're absolutely incredible.'

It's a relief not to have to justify, immediately, the more implausible aspects of the story I've just told. A relief to hear anything that isn't: *But you can't have seen that. It can't have happened. It's just not possible.*

'Where's Ed now?' I ask. 'Hasn't his school broken up yet?'

'No. Tomorrow they break up.'

Why is she saying nothing about the Orphan

Choir? Is she too non-judgemental to tell me that my story sounded like complete nonsense? I interrogate myself silently: did I definitely tell her? Could I have imagined telling her?

'But . . . Ed doesn't live with me, so . . .'. A shadow passes across Bethan's face. 'I won't be seeing him, even over Christmas. He lives with his father. Rod. We're separated.' She blinks away tears: more discreet ones than mine – tears that will take no for an answer. 'I know how painful it is to lose a child, Louise. Believe me. Death and abduction aren't the only ways it can happen, though they're the only ways people sympathise with. Ed's getting on with his life, getting on well at school. He seems happy. I see him every fortnight, for the weekend. No one can see that I've lost him except me. I mean, people know he lives with Rod, but . . . that's different from a tragedy, isn't it? In most people's eyes. It feels like a tragedy to me, though.'

'I'm so sorry,' I say. 'Did you . . . Could you . . .' I don't know how to ask without making her feel as if it's her fault, or as if I think it might be.

'I didn't fight Rod for custody, no. No point.'

'He'd win?'

'No, I think I would. But winning would be

losing.' She shakes her head, murmurs something under her breath. 'If I tell you, you'll think I'm spineless.'

'No, I won't.'

'Rod told me from the start – before we had kids, before we were engaged, even – that he'd never let any woman take his child away from him to live under another man's roof. He wouldn't have married me if I hadn't agreed. I was in love – I thought it was sweet, that it was fine because we were never going to split up. Rod was so serious about being a dad, he wanted it so much, but he wouldn't have gone into it if there was even a chance that some woman would separate him from his kids. It used to really worry him – even stopped him from having relationships for a while. Before he met me. We used to tease each other about it when things were okay between us. If Ed and I were nipping into town, Rod'd say jokily, "Taking my son away, are you? I seem to recall promising to kill any woman who did that." And I'd say, "Don't worry, you'll have him back in a couple of hours – you'll be poorer though, because we're going into town to get him a new coat. Lucky you've not sworn to kill anyone who spends too much of your hard-earned money!"'

Seeing my expression, Bethan says, 'I know it sounds awful but it was just one of our running gags. Neither of us thought the situation'd ever arise.' She falls silent.

'And when it did, you let Rod keep Ed because you knew it wasn't really a joke?' I ask.

'I don't know if he'd actually go as far as killing me. I'd rather not find out. He'd do something, that's for sure. Kill himself, maybe. I can't risk it. Anyway . . .' Bethan smiles determinedly and pats her lap with both hands: the signal for a cat to leap up into it, except there is no cat. 'You didn't come here to listen to me pouring my heart out with a tale of woe. We should be talking about you and what happened to you yesterday. I must say, that's something we *don't* have in common: I've never had a . . . an out-of-body experience like that. What do you think it means?'

'The Orphan Choir?' It feels so odd saying the words out loud. 'It wasn't an out-of-body experience exactly. I was in my body, and my mind, but they were . . . different. Everything was different. It's so hard to explain. But I do know what it means – I think. No, I *know*. But it'll sound crazy if I tell you. Crazier than what you've already heard.'

'Try me,' says Bethan. 'Like I said, I don't judge.'

'Then can you start now?' I am joking but not joking. Like Bethan's ex, Rod. 'I need someone to tell me if everything I'm thinking is a complete fantasy and I'm stark raving mad or if there could be any truth in it. I don't trust myself any more.'

'Go on.'

'I think the Orphan Choir's . . . visit was a warning. It was Joseph's choir.'

'You saw Joseph with them?' Bethan asks. 'You didn't mention that.'

'No, he wasn't one of them, but the three that told me their names – they're Saviour choirboys.'

'But one of them was a girl, you said – Lucinda Price.'

'Yes. Sorry.' Why is my brain not working properly? Bethan shouldn't know more about what happened yesterday than I do. 'The two boys, Alfie Speake and George Fairclough – they're choristers. Lucinda Price isn't, obviously – no girls are allowed in Saviour's choir. She must be one of the choirboys' sisters. In fact, all the girls I saw must be. That's why it's the Orphan Choir – what else can it mean? If the choirboys are orphans, their parents must be dead. If their parents are dead, that would make their sisters orphans too.'

Jagged and silver in the night; blue-white eyes shining. Wide black mouths scream-singing.

'So ... you said you thought it was a warning?' Bethan prompts.

'Sometimes Saviour's choir sings in other places apart from the college chapel. Not often, but it happens. In February they're going to be singing at St Paul's in London. They're going by coach, with the choirmaster, Dr Freeman. There's a separate coach booked to take parents and families.' Since yesterday, my mind has been full of all the terrible things that might happen to that coach. Will it plunge off a hill road and crash into the valley below, killing everyone on impact? There are no hills between Cambridge and London, so probably not. Will it overturn on the M11 and burst into flames?

'And you're worried it's going to crash and kill you all?' Bethan asks.

'Not me, not Stuart. We're not going to be on that coach. I need to warn all the other parents, but how can I? They won't believe me. You don't believe me, do you? I won't blame you at all if you don't.

I'd rather be wrong. I'd rather be mad! At least if I'm the crazy one then the rest of the world still makes sense!'

'The girls, though,' Bethan says, frowning. 'That's where your theory falls down.'

'What do you mean?'

'Well, if they're sisters of choirboys, they'd be on the second coach too, wouldn't they? The parents' and families' coach, the one laid on to transport the audience. Not the one that's taking the choirboys. So –'

'They wouldn't be alive and orphaned. They'd be dead along with the parents.' I finish Bethan's sentence for her. 'Yes, I thought about that. But...maybe not everyone on the second coach died? Or some of the choirboys' sisters might have been left at home with a sitter, a grandparent – maybe those girls are the ones I saw and heard in the Orphan Choir.'

'"Dies", you mean. Not "died". None of these parents and sisters are dead yet, are they?'

I appreciate Bethan's matter-of-fact approach. She's the one making it possible for us to continue this conversation, not me.

'Should I warn them?' I ask. 'We're going to

Cambridge this Friday for a Choral Evensong. I'll see all the choir parents there.'

Bethan rubs the palm of her left hand with the thumb of her right as she thinks about it. 'I don't think you need to warn anybody,' she says eventually. 'Why wouldn't the Orphan Choir warn the other parents, if they warned you? To be honest . . .' She stops. 'Do you want to know what I really think?'

I nod. A grey stone of dread has started to form at the base of my throat. I need to be right about this. I know I can avoid that coach trip; I need it to be that and nothing else that I have to avoid.

In case I can't.

'I think it was a warning, like you say, but nothing to do with a coach trip,' says Bethan. 'I honestly don't think all the choir families are going to die on the way to St Paul's Cathedral. I don't believe in ghosts or anything supernatural like that – do you?'

'No. Nor premonitions, not usually, but . . . I can't deny what happened to me yesterday. It definitely happened.'

'Yes. It happened in here' – she taps the side of her head with her finger – 'because you desperately want your son back. You want and need to get him out of Saviour College School – you've been miserable since he started there. *That's* the warning. You're missing Joe so much, you're seeing orphaned choirboys who've been tragically separated from their parents. You don't like this Dr Freeman, or trust him further than you can throw him...The mind's a powerful machine, Louise. It can do an awful lot to us that we don't understand.'

'I know that.'

She's wrong. The Orphan Choir means more than she thinks it does. It didn't come from inside my head.

She's wrong because of the girls.

Why would my mind produce girls, when the choir from which I am desperate to extricate my son is a boys-only choir?

'Your subconscious is panicking, Louise – that's what's going on. Here at Swallowfield you've got Joe with you and you're happy, but this holiday period can't last for ever. Subconsciously, you know that the start of term's going to be even more painful because you've had Joe back for a bit – and soon you'll have to say goodbye to him again.' Bethan shrugs. 'Or else it's this Dr Freeman – maybe you don't like him for a different reason from the one you assume. He might not be fit to look after children – he might be a monster.'

No. Ivan Freeman isn't a monster; he is someone whose wishes and self-interest clash with mine, that's all. That's enough.

'Maybe on a gut-instinct level, you've worked out that you need to get Joe away from Dr Freeman double quick.'

My son's name is Joseph. Not Joe.

'I don't believe in ghosts, but I definitely believe dodgy people can give off danger vibes that can make alarm bells ring,' Bethan says. 'And so can situations. I don't know if it's separation from Joe you're afraid of or Dr Freeman, but whichever it is, you should heed the warning your brain's trying to give you – all the warnings you've had since Joe started school – and move him to a different school, a day school. Get him back for good and I promise you, you won't be seeing any more choirs of orphans hovering above lakes.'

Wrong. I will see and hear them again. Until I understand.

I intend to get Joseph back for good, of course, but she's wrong about the rest. I would say so, but I can no longer motivate myself to tell her what I'm thinking.

I stand up. 'Thank you,' I say. No swearing this time. 'I need to get home.'

𝄞

Outside Bethan's house, there is a boy. He has been waiting for me, barefoot on the wooden bridge: a choirboy in a dark red cassock, tall and thin with a prominent Adam's apple. His hair is blond and fine, his eyes blue-grey. He smiles at me, then starts to sing the first hymn I ever heard my son sing:

> *Dear Lord and Father of mankind,*
> *Forgive our foolish ways.*
> *Re-clothe us in our rightful mind,*
> *In purer lives thy service find*
> *In deeper reverence, praise . . .*

As he sings, his skin fades around the black hole of his open mouth.

I should be scared, but I'm not. He is not my son.

He's nobody's son. He's an orphan.

Was. Now he's gone, his unfinished song is gone, and there's nothing and no one on the bridge apart from me and a few stones and dried-up brown leaves.

10

The chaplain of Saviour College, whose last service this is, has a serious cold and should be in bed with a mug of Lemsip, not here in this chilly echo-chamber. He is doing his best, spluttering over some of his words.

Seeing him walk into the chapel reminded me that I didn't respond to any of Alexis Grant's emails about the leaving present that she'd decided we were all going to buy him, communally. I didn't even read them. Ours is probably the only family that hasn't contributed. I'm not even sure what the present is. A quick glance at Alexis's first round-robin email on the subject told me everything I needed to know:

it was something complicated and partially home-made that involved taking one's child's fingerprints and then posting them to Alexis, having first taken care not to smudge them and made sure the envelope was hardbacked to avoid it getting bent in transit ... I stopped reading when it became apparent that more effort would be involved than I was prepared to put in.

It shouldn't matter. I shouldn't be here. Neither should Stuart. Neither should Joseph. Part of the reason I ignored and deleted all of Alexis's emails is because, in my mind, we were already gone: an ex-Saviour family, with no further need to be involved in choir business on any level. We were gone, as far as I was concerned, from the moment I first saw the Orphan Choir and fully understood that Joseph had to leave.

Yet there he is: singing.

Yet here we all are: in Saviour's chapel, as if nothing has changed, with Alexis beaming her stony disapproval at me from the pews opposite. I try to beam back the words 'I am not really here,' but it doesn't deter her.

Until the last minute – until half an hour before we set off from Swallowfield – I believed that I would find a way out of coming tonight. Then Stuart appeared with his car keys in his hand, and Joseph was standing next to him with his coat on, and I saw that I had misled myself yet again. There was never going to be a way out.

That's when I realised: maybe we need to go back and face the college and the choir once more, or twice more, before we can sever all ties. If everything happens for a reason – and they say it does, don't they? – then perhaps it will do me good to sit here, listen to the service, appreciate what's being discarded. Perhaps this, like the visit from the Orphan Choir, is happening for a very good reason – something to do with the difference between achieving closure in an active way and going into hiding like a coward.

For the first time at a Saviour service, I scan the faces of boys who aren't my son, as they sing the Magnificat. I steel myself for my least favourite line.

. . . and the rich he hath sent empty away . . .

Normally I can't tear my eyes away from Joseph, but today I am keen to see Alfie Speake and George

Fairclough. And the Price boy, Lucinda's brother.

Except ... none of them is here today.

That's peculiar. Saviour choirboys have it drummed into them from day one that they must attend every service unless they're seriously ill. I wonder if they have caught the chaplain's lurgy. Leaning in to Stuart, I whisper, 'Three boys missing. Not seen that before.'

'What are you talking about?' he says. 'They're all there.'

'Alfie Speake and George Fairclough aren't.'

The Magnificat finishes. 'Let us now offer to God our prayers and petitions,' says the chaplain in his cold-muffled voice. 'Let us pray for all those who are going to be alone this Christmas, those who have lost a loved one this year and will miss them on Christmas Day, those without adequate food and shelter, those suffering in the war-torn parts of the world – in Syria, the Gaza Strip ...'

'Who?' Stuart whispers.

'He can't mention everyone in the Gaza Strip by name,' I say.

'No, I meant Alfie ... who did you say?'

'Alfie Speake, and George Fairclough. And ... what's the name of the Price boy?'

'Who are you talking about?' Stuart stares at me oddly.

'Ssh.' I nod in Joseph's direction. I don't want us to embarrass him. This service and one more and then he's out of here for good. I can't wait.

'We pray for the recently and prematurely deceased,' intones the chaplain. 'For the repose of the souls of Cordelia Overton, Martin Moss, Walter Hepworth, Carole Waugh, Gary Donald. Lord in thy mercy...'

'Hear our prayer,' I mutter. Playing my part for the second-to-last time.

'Lou,' says Stuart.

'What?' I whisper.

'There's no one called Price in the choir.'

I turn to face him. What's he talking about? 'Of course there is.' I roll my eyes at him. 'I promise you, there is. You never know anyone's name.'

'We pray for individuals who have asked for our prayers, and for those for whom prayers have been asked by others – Katie Nally, Felix and Antonia Blackwood, Maureen and Roger. Lord in thy mercy...'

'Hear our prayer.'

'I know that there's no boy with the surname

Price in the choir,' Stuart persists. 'There's no Alfie Speake or George Fairclough either.'

'What are you talking about? Of course there is.'

'No. There isn't.' There are tears in my husband's eyes. They scare me, and I don't want to be scared, not after believing and hoping that I was well on the way to leaving fear behind. That solitary orphan choirboy on Bethan's bridge, outside The Hush . . . As we drove to Cambridge, it suddenly dawned on me what he meant. One choirboy, not lots. Singing softly, not screaming out the words. And he faded almost immediately. Another warning, but a milder one — more of a gentle reminder: 'Don't forget. I know you won't, but just in case . . .'

'Look,' Stuart says, bringing me back to now. 'Everybody's here — all the choristers. Count them. How many boys are there in Saviour's choir?'

No. I don't want to do this.

'How many, Lou?'

'Sixteen.'

'And how many are here this evening? Count them.'

I don't want to.

'Do it,' Stuart insists.

One, two, three. Four, five, six. Joseph is number seven. *Eight, nine. Teneleventwelvethirteenfourteenfifteensixteen.*

'But ... I don't understand,' I whisper. Alfie and George aren't here. Where are they? How can there still be sixteen choirboys?

There were hundreds. In the Orphan Choir. Hundreds. I saw all their faces.

Only sixteen in Saviour's choir. Only ever sixteen.

I gasp at the shock of this revelation as the chaplain says, 'On the anniversaries of their deaths, we pray for Adele Nolan, Jared Pazdur...'

'Lou? You okay?' Stuart grips my arm. 'You've gone pale.'

I'll be fine. I'll work out what it means and then I'll be okay.

'...Tamsin, Fluffy Heywood, Damian Cricklade...'

I'd be better if the chaplain would stop listing dead people. It's macabre. Did all of them really die on 21 December, or have some people rounded their loved ones' death anniversaries up or down to the nearest Saviour chapel service? Is Fluffy Heywood a person or a former pet rabbit, for Christ's sake?

'...Agnes Barrow, Patricia Jervis and Gillian Voss. Lord in thy mercy...'

Hear

our

prayer

I press my eyes shut. *No. No. It's not true.* He can't have said it. *Patricia Jervis.* I open my mouth, not sure if I'm going to breathe or scream.

'Lou — what is it?' Stuart asks.

He must be talking about a different person: someone who's been dead for at least a year, not someone who works for the council, who came to my house twice. *Pat isn't dead. She isn't dead. She's Pat, not Patricia — short for Patricia, but she said everyone calls her Pat. This is a terrible mistake.*

'Out,' I say, standing up. 'Now.' I have to get out of here, away from this endless remembering of death. Have to get back to Swallowfield, back to safety. Stuart tries to pull me down. I shake his hand off my arm and run across the black-and-white tiled floor of the chapel to Joseph, with my arms stretched out in front of me. 'Mrs Beeston?' Dr Freeman says. 'What . . . ?'

It feels like hours before I am close enough to grab my shocked son. I hug his warm body against mine. 'We're leaving!' I shout. If I can make it to the door and out into the courtyard, we'll be all right.

Run. Run.

&

'Where did you take him?' I call out when I hear the front door close. I yell it twice more before Stuart appears in the lounge. He's taken too long; that must mean he's taken Joseph far away, irretrievably far. I'm sitting on the floor at The Boundary, in the corner of the room, my knees drawn up to my chest, pressing the sides of my back into a right angle of walls. Sitting on a chair or on the sofa I would feel too exposed. I'd like someone to wrap my whole body in a blanket, round and round, so that I can't move. That would make me feel safer.

'Where did I take him?' Stuart snaps. 'Where do you think I took him? To Bethan's house, like we agreed.'

'No! I don't agree.'

'But ... you were the one who rang Bethan and asked her if she'd have him overnight!' My husband's face is grey. I am destroying him. It's not me, though; I have to make him see that. It's not my fault, none of it. If I rang Bethan – and Stuart's right, I did – that must mean I want Joseph to be there, with her.

'I don't think you took him to Bethan's,' I say

slowly. 'I bet you took him back to Cambridge, didn't you? Handed him over to Dr Freeman!'

'Lou, I've been gone forty minutes. To Cambridge and back's two and a half hours. It's a bloody nightmare finding Bethan's place in the dark. I also—'

'Get him back!' I sob. 'I want Joseph! I want my son!'

'Lou.' Stuart sits down next to me on the floor. 'We discussed this. Remember? The drive home was bad enough – do you want to traumatise him permanently? We need to talk, and Joseph needs not to be within earshot... Look, he's fine with Bethan. He'll be asleep by now.'

'Bury me behind the walls,' I say. 'Bury me under the floorboards. Let me die. I can't bear this any more.'

'Stop it! You sound crazy.'

'I *am* crazy!'

'Look, we're going to try and make sense of all this, all right? All of it. Even though it makes no fucking sense whatsoever. Pat Jervis – the Pat Jervis you claim to have met twice, in our house – is dead.'

'No!'

'*Yes*, Louise. I've been sitting in the car with my

phone for the last quarter of an hour, doing a bit of research. Patricia Jervis, worked for Cambridge City Council's environmental health department. Murdered on the twenty-first of December 2009. She was investigating a noise complaint, went to the house in question to try to reason with the party animal who lived there. He pushed her off a fourth-floor roof terrace.'

I need him to stop talking. I can't breathe while he's talking.

'She broke her neck and back.'

Which is why she walks funny, rocking from side to side. I think back to my telephone conversation with Doug Minns. I asked to speak to Pat. He didn't tell me she was dead.

He must have been being tactful. Easier, less shocking, to say, 'Let me help you instead,' or words to that effect, than to say to a stranger, 'I'm sorry, my colleague was murdered some years back. Can I help you at all?'

'She's dead, Lou. Which means she didn't turn up to our house in the middle of the night, and you didn't meet her and speak to her. So . . . is there anything you want to tell me?'

'You think I'm *lying*? Why would I make that up?'

'You tell me. While you're at it, why don't you tell me who Alfie Speake and George Fairclough are?'

'I . . .'

'Saviour choirboys, are they?' Stuart says, his voice leaden with sarcasm.

'No. I . . . I thought they were, but . . . no. They belong to a different choir.'

'A *different* choir? Jesus Christ, Louise . . .'

'They belong to the Orphan Choir.'

'Oh, orphans now, are they?'

I don't understand why he's being so cruel to me.

'Shall I tell you what I think?' he says. 'I think you've developed some kind of . . . twisted obsession with death. You *knew* Pat Jervis was dead. How much time do you spend on the Internet, Googling macabre deaths?'

'I don't know what you're talking about.'

'If I look at the browsing history on your laptop, I wonder what I'll find,' Stuart says knowingly.

'Whatever you suspect me of, you're wrong,' I tell him. I'm exhausted; I need to stop, to sleep for ever, but I can't stop. I must carry on. It isn't up to me.

'Alfie Speake was a Cambridge chorister, like Joseph, except at King's, not Saviour,' Stuart says. 'There was a documentary about him on telly two months ago. As if you don't know all this.'

I don't.

'Tell me,' I say.

'Do we really have to go through this charade?' Stuart sighs. 'All right, then. Alfie was a composer – a musical child prodigy. He died in 1983, aged nine: his father accidentally reversed his car over him.'

Oh, yes. I remember this now. Stuart's right about Alfie.

'George Fairclough died in 1979 of leukaemia, aged twelve,' I say, not knowing how I know this – only that I do. 'George was a brilliant singer too, though he wasn't in a choir. He wasn't well known, wasn't any kind of celebrity apart from in private, where he was, very much so.'

He was picked for the Orphan Choir because his was one of the best voices. It didn't matter that he wasn't famous and had never been a chorister at an Oxbridge college.

Stuart stares at me, confused.

'George's parents used to invite all their friends round for musical evenings,' I tell him. 'His mother would play the piano while George sang. It became a regular thing – everyone looked forward to it.'

'How do you know that, if he wasn't famous?' Stuart asks quietly. 'I couldn't find any useful Google results for George Fairclough.'

'And Lucinda Price – she died last year, aged ten. In Prestatyn. Her uncle raped and murdered her.'

'Right, just . . . stop this now!'

'He was supposed to be babysitting. She was a brilliant singer, Lucinda was. Won the Eisteddfod two years running.'

'The . . . what?'

It doesn't matter. A warm calm settles over me as I let the knowledge sink in. I was wrong before, so wrong, but it doesn't matter. I see it all now and there's no point fighting. There's no avoiding it.

The Orphan Choir. They're all dead. Children who were talented singers. Children who, wherever they are now, have no parents because their parents are still here: in this world. That's why they're orphans. Their parents, still alive, are lost to them.

Boys and girls. Saviour College choir, with its archaic traditions, excludes girls. The Orphan Choir excludes no child who can sing as beautifully as Alfie and George and Lucinda.

SOPHIE HANNAH

*And Joseph. And the boy who sang to me outside Bethan's
house . . .*

I shiver. Wrap my arms round my knees. Stuart
is saying something but I can't hear him. I'm
consumed by my own thoughts, and I'm so close
now. I can allow myself to remember, to know, to
see.

Pat Jervis, pressing her fingertip against the
glass of my light-blocked lounge window . . . Me,
looking at my reflection in the same black window
later, feeling strongly that something was wrong,
but it wasn't — not then. It was wrong before, when
Pat looked, when I saw her looking, saw what she
saw. That's what I half-remembered when I stood
where she had stood: the lounge was reflected in
the window, everything in the lounge but her. She
didn't see herself there.

She wasn't there.

That's why she presses her finger against panes
of glass and mirrors. She can't see her reflection.
She touches to check that the surface that ought to
reflect her presence is there. Wonders why, if it is,
she can't see herself in it.

*She doesn't understand that she's dead. Not fully. I'm the
same.*

302

No. I'm not dead. I'm still alive.

Think, Louise. Think hard.

The Orphan Choir didn't mean what I thought it meant: it wasn't about dead parents – that wasn't why the children were orphans. I got it the wrong way round. I saw dead children singing above the lake. Dead, like Alfie Speake. Dead, like...

No.

'What's that noise?' Stuart asks. 'Someone's playing...' He stops to listen, frowning.

'She warned me.'

'Who?'

'Pat Jervis. She told me not to buy a house here. She knew the danger wasn't in Cambridge.'

I replay her words in my mind: *I know you shouldn't drive to the Culver Valley. Don't do it, Louise. Stay here.*

'Louise! What's that singing? I can hear boys singing.'

'It's the Orphan Choir.' Who else would it be?

Slowly, Stuart walks towards the French doors. Opens them.

There's no hurry. It's all much too late.

The children are brighter tonight, glowing gold and silver, huge radiant eyes and endless black mouths like tunnels to purest nowhere.

They're singing their favourite: 'O Come, O Come, Emmanuel'.

'Joseph,' Stuart whispers. He looks tiny beneath the enormous jagged moon of children. Powerless. As we both are and have always been. 'Joseph's there.'

I join him on the terrace. My feet are bare, as I need them to be. 'Yes,' I say. 'And Ed, look, next to him. Ed's his best friend in his new choir.' The blond boy I saw on the bridge that leads to Bethan's house, with the prominent Adam's apple.

'Ed?'

'Bethan's son.' Somehow, I know what happened to him too, just like I know all about Alfie Speake and George Fairclough.

Murdered by his father, Rod. Strangled with the lead of a laptop computer after Bethan said she wanted a divorce and really meant it this time. It wasn't enough for Rod to be his son's primary carer; he had to punish Bethan, had to deprive her of a son altogether.

I'm not angry that she didn't tell me. I understand. I would never have let Joseph go anywhere near her or her house if I'd known the truth.

'Lou, we've got to get Joseph. I . . . I don't think he's safe at Bethan's.'

'Joseph's dead,' I tell him. 'He's dead because Ed

needed a friend.' I wonder if Bethan understands why she did it.

'No!' Stuart says. 'Don't say that!'

'You know it's true. You just don't want to face it.'

'Shut up! I'm going to get my son back!'

I remember that I used to say that. Used to think it, all the time. Had no idea what it might come to mean.

Stuart disappears round the side of the house. I hear him unlock the car. *Good.* I want him gone. I can't do what I have to do with him here. He would stop me; he's still in denial. I need it to be just me and the choir. They know what has to happen next.

My son is lying on the bottom bunk of a bed that once belonged to a murdered boy. Poisoned, not strangled; Bethan's a coward.

Eyes closed. Pale skin. Wearing his favourite pyjamas: the ones with a grey smiling shark on the top.

And Stuart is driving, and crying. Soon he'll be running...

I don't want him to see what I see, but how can I stop him?

Across the bridge, pushing past Bethan, up the

stairs, second door on the left; he'll be drawn to the room Joseph's in. He will turn on the light and be blinded by pain.

I don't want him to fall to his knees and howl, but he will. I can't stop it.

My son is a murdered boy, lying on another murdered boy's bottom bunk.

But. The Orphan Choir would not still be singing to me if there was nothing I could do. They are showing me, Joseph is showing me, that he doesn't need to be an orphan. Not at all. I can join him if I want to.

How could I not want to? He's my only child.

I walk through the bodies of long-dead children to the edge of the lake. Descend the steps that one of Swallowfield's gardeners cut into the bank, one by one. The children sing to me as I go down.

THREE

II

The antechapel is cold, as I knew it would be. Grey stone everywhere. Behind the closed wooden doors, I have no doubt that the chapel proper is colder. I have never seen or sat inside it; this is the first time I have been here, at the invitation of the choirmaster.

I don't know who decided, and when, that religion and central heating were incompatible.

Actually, it was more of a summons than an invitation. I had no choice but to attend at the given time. He'd have come for me if I hadn't.

It's odd that I don't know his name.

Still, it is better this way round. I can afford to let things happen as they will, knowing I'll get the outcome I want. With Dr Freeman there was so much resistance; I had to make such an effort, had to hatch plans and strategise. Today, a new choirmaster will offer me what Dr Freeman never would have, however long I'd waited, and I will have to make no effort at all.

The wooden doors open with a creak. He is on the other side of them and stays where he is; doesn't walk towards me. 'Mrs Beeston.'

'Yes.' I approach. Close as I can. I want to catch a glimpse of Joseph inside. I can hear him singing the Nunc Dimittis. I hear all the voices – Alfie's, Ed's – but especially Joseph's.

'You know why I asked you to come?'

'I think so, yes.'

'Joseph's voice is exceptional and he's a hard worker. We'll be very sorry to lose him, but ... he has you now. He no longer meets our eligibility criteria, and there are other boys ... And girls,' the choirmaster adds, as if he's surprised to have remembered this detail. I would like to ask him if, before, he led a boys-only choir like Saviour's, but I would feel inappropriate if I did. There's a lot that no one talks about. Ever.

'I'm only sorry to lose Joseph so soon,' he

says. 'Obviously all the children have to move on eventually when their parents come, and it's always a blessing for a parent to arrive, however unexpectedly, especially a mother, but... well, Joseph's very special. As you must know, of course. I'll be sad to see him go.'

'Thank you.' I smile at him.

'Mum?'

I look down and find Joseph standing next to me. 'Darling,' I whisper. 'I missed you.'

'I missed you too,' he says. 'Can we go home?'

'Yes, of course.'

It is true. I am going to take my son home. Finally, there is no one who can stop me.

𝄞

The scaffolding is still up, the plastic sheeting still wrapped around our house on Weldon Road. Inside, though, it's brighter than it's ever been: a silver-white glare. So bright that, at first, I can't see Joseph. I have to let my eyes adjust. I squeeze his hand and he squeezes back. I will never let go of him again. Everything will be all right. Everything has to be all right now, because now is for ever.

'Mummy?'

'Yes, darling?' He hasn't called me Mummy for a long time. It was Mum, as soon as he started primary school.

'Will I still see Ed, now that I've left the choir?'

How do I answer him? I have no idea how this kind of thing works, no idea where to go or what to do.

Perhaps, because this is home, there will be no more going and doing. I will have to work it out.

'I don't know, darling. Maybe. I'll know soon. I'll sort it out, I promise.'

'Will you ask Ed's mummy?'

'Ed's mummy?' I have no idea what to say to this.

'She's coming soon, you know. Ed told me today.'

I nod, distracted, as the shine from the window pulls me towards it. When Pat pressed her fingertip against it, it was black. Not any more. I put my finger where hers was and, for a second, the brightness clears and I see my reflection in the glass. There's someone standing behind me.

It's Bethan. She opens her mouth as if to tell me something, then fades to a pinprick of movement in the surrounding stillness before disappearing altogether.

'Mummy?' Joseph tugs at my sleeve.

'Yes, Joseph?'

'When will Daddy come?'

'I don't know. Soon, I hope.' I wonder, as I say this, if it's true.

Give us light in the night season, we beseech thee, O
    Lord,
and grant that our rest may be without sin,
and our waking to thy service;
that we may come in peace and safety
to the waking of the great day;
through Jesus Christ our Lord.
Amen.

Let us bless the Lord.
Thanks be to God.

The Lord Almighty grant us a quiet night and a perfect
    end.
Amen.

All remain standing.

MY RELATIONSHIP WITH GHOSTS

I have always loved ghost stories, for the same reason that I've always loved crime fiction: the suspense. In both genres, the reader or viewer knows that something untoward is afoot, but doesn't know exactly what or why, and the main thing driving her on through the narrative is the desire to find out and solve the mystery.

Though I haven't read nearly as many ghostly novels as I've read detective stories, my strong impression from the few that I *have* read is that the overwhelming majority of ghost stories are mysteries. There might be some supernatural fiction in which the ghost is upfront, announcing himself and declaring his agenda right from the start, but if there is then I certainly haven't stumbled across it. All the ghosts I encounter in films and in literature are as sneaky and elusive as murderers who wish to avoid exposure. Even those with grudges that border on obsession seem oddly reluctant to rant explicitly about their various beefs with the living; they all seem to feel it's more effective to make a door slam shut or a floorboard creak, hoping to get their message across in a long-drawn-out and incredibly indirect way instead. This makes no sense, when you think about it. If I were dead and angry, and had magic non-earthly powers, I would defy ghostly convention and stand next to those who'd wronged me, screaming, 'You poisonous git! I'll never forgive you! Just you wait and see how many of your relatives I'm going to kill and maim before the weekend!' All right, it's not subtle, but since I'd probably be shimmery and transparent at the time of yelling, I like to think I could achieve some pretty devastating effects by combining verbal straightforwardness with physical ethereality.

Perhaps this is why I so admired the recent and utterly brilliant Hammer film adaptation of Susan Hill's equally brilliant novel *The Woman in Black*. The ghost in that movie is a comparatively direct communicator. At one point, she writes on a wall in capital letters, 'YOU COULD HAVE SAVED HIM', and, in doing so, helpfully reveals what, precisely, she's cross about. (Admittedly, she is less forthcoming about why she chooses to vent her anger on the innocent; I'd be interested to see what she might write on a wall on the subject of legitimate targets and collateral damage, but that's another story.)

Like all my favourite ghost and horror films – *Dead of Night, The Others, The Innocents, The Haunting, The Shining, The Sixth Sense* – *The Woman in Black* was completely terrifying from start to finish; I watched most of it from behind my woolly scarf. I was sitting next to an elderly couple in the cinema, and throughout the film they regularly asked me if I was okay. I wasn't, and nor did I want to be. There is no point in a fictional ghost if he or she doesn't frighten the life out of you.

Which is why, when I was invited to write a novella for the new Hammer imprint, my first thought was 'Ooh, yes, but it must be terrifying.' And mysterious too – because all my favourite stories are driven by mysteries and the need to find out the truth and outwit the cunning author who is annoyingly trying to withhold it for as long as possible. So I resisted the temptation to redefine the genre by creating a loud-mouthed ghost who yells at people obsessively and informatively, and tried as hard as I could to frighten myself instead. Just as, in my crime writing, I have always resisted the (sometimes very strong) temptation to write a psychological thriller that begins with the heroine receiving a phone call from someone from her shady past to whom she hasn't spoken for twenty years, and immediately announcing to her happy middle-class family in a cheery voice, 'Hey, it's So-and-So — remember, the one I committed that murder with twenty years ago? Remember, I *did* tell you ...'

Sophie Hannah
January 2013

About Hammer

Hammer is the most well-known film brand in the UK, having made over 150 feature films which have been terrifying and thrilling audiences worldwide for generations.

Whilst synonymous with horror and the genre-defining classics it produced in the 1950s to 1970s, Hammer was recently rebooted in the film world as the home of "Smart Horror", with the critically acclaimed *Let Me In* and *The Woman in Black*. With *The Woman in Black: Angel of Death* scheduled for 2014, Hammer has been re-born.

Hammer's literary legacy is also now being revived through its new partnership with Arrow Books. This series features original novellas by some of today's most celebrated authors, as well as classic stories from nearly a century of production.

In 2013 Hammer Arrow will publish books by Melvin Burgess, Julie Myerson and Sophie Hannah as well as a novelisation of the forthcoming *The Woman in Black: Angel of Death*, continuing a programme that began with bestselling novellas from Helen Dunmore and Jeanette Winterson. Beautifully produced and written to read in a single sitting, Hammer Arrow books are perfect for readers of quality contemporary fiction.

For more information on Hammer
visit: www.hammerfilms.com or
www.facebook.com/hammerfilms

IF YOU LIKED *THE ORPHAN CHOIR*
THEN YOU MIGHT ENJOY *THE WOMAN IN BLACK:*
ANGEL OF DEATH

**The fully authorised chilling sequel to Susan Hill's bestselling
ghost-story, *The Woman in Black*.**

1940: World War Two

A group of school children and their teacher escape the London
Blitz and arrive at a lonely, desolate house – where someone is
waiting for them.

She is someone the children cannot see, but she is far more
dangerous and deadly than the German bombs.
She is ...

The Woman in Black

**SOON TO BE A MAJOR FILM STARRING
JEREMY IRVINE AND PHOEBE FOX**

Look out for Sophie Hannah's next unnerving
psychological thriller

THE TELLING ERROR

Stuck in a traffic jam on her way to deliver her son's forgotten
sports kit to school, Nicki Clements sees a face she hoped never to
see again. It's definitely him, the same police officer; he's stopping
all the cars on Elmhirst Road one by one, talking to every driver.
Keen to avoid him, Nicki does a U-turn and takes a long and
inconvenient detour, praying he won't notice her panicky escape.

He doesn't, but a CCTV camera does, as Nicki finds out when
detectives pull her in for questioning the next day in connection
with the murder of Damon Blundy, a controversial newspaper
columnist and resident of Elmhirst Road.

Nicki can't answer any of the baffling questions detectives fire at
her. She has no idea why a killer might sharpen nine knives at the
murder scene, then use two blunt ones to kill, in a way that involves
no stabbing or spilling of blood. She doesn't know what
'HE IS NO LESS DEAD' means, or why the murderer painted it on
the wall of Blundy's study. And she can't explain her desire to avoid
Elmhirst Road on the day in question without revealing the secret
that could ruin her life. Because, although Nicki is not guilty of
murder, she is far from innocent . . .

Coming out in hardback and ebook in 2014

**HODDER &
STOUGHTON**